THE MANY LIVES OF DEATH

Ryan Kapsar

This is dedicated to Davianne.

Thank you for your love and support.

Gary, Mild Mannered, Death

Gary was in the middle of his warehouse discussing supply constrains with one of his shift supervisors. The warehouse was clean and orderly. This was a Lean shop, after all. His wife was a few feet away talking with Gary's CFO.

He heard an alarm sound. Someone shouted, "Loose forklift!"

He turned to the sound of the yell and saw a forklift barreling down on his wife. He turned and dove pushing her out of the way. He jumped to his feet only to get impaled by the lift. His wife wailed. People shouted. He drifted off into darkness. He felt content that he lived a life well lived.

"Man, I'm glad you're here to celebrate the good work that we've done. We've really helped pull our community out of poverty. The jobs we've brought, are good paying jobs, with good health insurance. We're actually making a difference." Gary said. He leaned back and soaked in the view. He was at the Black Rock resort in Maui.

The man look back at him and nodded. He took a sip of the Pina Colada in front of him. He nodded at the flavor. "You did excellent work, Gary. You've gotta let that go, though."

"What do you mean? 'Let that go'" Gary asked

"You aren't that man any more. That man is gone."

"No! That man isn't gone! I'm ready to get back to work. We have more work to do. Lots to do. Plenty to do. I'm not ready to put the work down."

"Gary, do you remember how you got here?"

"Of course, we took a plane, then a car. Simple."

The man shook his head. "No, how did you get here, this time. That's how you got there before. This time. Where do you last remember you were?"

Gary paused. He glanced about. "I was discussing something with Alberto."

"Yea, you just suddenly ended up here. Like in a dream, right?"

Gary nodded. He fiddled with his straw.

The man continued, "Like a dream. Do you know who I am?"

"I imagined you at first as Si, my brother, but you're not Si. I, uh, I don't know you."

"Then let me introduce myself. I am called many things, but I'll just cut to the chase. I'm the Grim Reaper. I am Death. Or at least an aspect of Death. It's a pleasure to meet you," Death reached out his hand, Gary absently shook it.

"Please call me Tim. It was my name, when I was alive." Death said.

"I'm dead?"

"Yes."

"No."

"I'm 'fraid so."

"How can this be?"

"Someone let loose a forklift. You sacrificed yourself to save your wife. A very noble thing to do."

"Did she live?"

"It seemed like it."

"But you don't know?"

Death leaned back in his chair, he took a sip of his drink. He waved his hand, "This," he sighed and started again. "Look, time is different here. For all I know, you died before me. I could spend the next hundred years with you here, but still greet the soul the died at the same time as you, as if no time had passed."

"Why would we spend 100 years together?"

"Because, if you don't leave all your earthly concerns behind, you'd become a ghost, and I can't allow that."

"Why not?"

"Because, then you'd never go into the great beyond." He gestured towards the sea. The sun was setting. Gary could just make out a doorway through the glare.

"So. Tim, I'm not sure what I need to put down. I lived a great full life. I even died a hero. I feel good about my life." He smiled at Tim.

Tim nodded, "Yes, I can see that. You just want more of life. Then again who doesn't."

"What's out there? In the great beyond."Gary asked.

"I don't know. They don't tell us." Tim replied.

"Why haven't you moved through the great beyond?"

"I'm waiting for a replacement. I've had about all of this I can. I'm ready to move on. This place, though, this needs a caretaker. Someone, like you."

"Me?"

"Yea. Someone with no weights to let go. That's a great listener, but craves more. This is a chance for you to do that."

Tim pulled off a bracelet and placed it on the table.

"What's this?" Gary asked.

"This, is what makes me Death. There are more than one Death, and with the way Time works, our time will overlap, I'm sure." He gave Gary a warm smile.

Gary picked up the bracelet, "I just put it on and I'm Death?"

"Yep. Just that simple. It'll do the hard part for you."

Gary placed it on his wrist, "Good luck Tim."

Gary was suddenly at a small camp fire. A man was speaking. He was a small rugged man. His ribs were showing. He held a clay thrown cup in one hand.

"Xerwa, she humiliated me. She always went from furs to furs. It was too much. I had to kill Irxa, he was enjoying her too much. As if Xerwa was his woman."

Gary nodded as the man's life flooded into his mind. It had been a short brutal life. Pilxa was his name. "Irxa certainly overstepped. You know that Xerwa was doing what was only within her rights."

"Xerwa, could have shared furs with anyone. Irxa coerced her!" He spat into the fire.

"There was no way Xerwa could have been coerced, she would have gone to the Women's Circle. Irxa would have been dealt with."

Pilxa glared at Gary.

"If she had gone to the Women's Circle, I'd be talking with Irxa instead of you. Do you remember how you got here?"

Pilxa's eyes widened, "No. I cannot have lost to Irxa? No." He sobbed into his hands.

Gary consoled the man.

Eventually Pilxa looked back at Gary, "You are right, white man. Thank you for helping me understand. I didn't lose to Irxa. I betrayed Xerwa's trust and that sealed my fate. I died at her hand. It was just that I died."

Gary noticed the cave to his left. "Why don't you rest now. No one will bother you."

The man stood and shuffled towards the cave entrance. As he got closer he became less and less coherent. He disappeared as he stepped through.

Gary was in a dimly lit bar. It was a beautiful bar, clearly an expensive. His hand was cooled by an icy Old Fashioned. He looked at the man across from him.

"I still can't believe she did it. That she made me part of her scheme." Ralph muttered into his drink. He looked up at Gary and dropped his glass.

The man's life flooded Gary. This man was a District Attorney, then Governor, then President.

"Are you ok, Ralph?" Gary asked.

"You're, you're dead!"

"Yes, I am. I greet those who have recently died. Which means, you've died too."

"Fuck, no. I was on my way." He had a far off look as spoke.

"Well, you can take as much time as you'd like to process it. This is your time."

"What do you mean?"

"Before you're able to leave the bar, as it were, you need to unburden yourself of everything."

"If I refuse?"

Gary shrugged, "It's no matter to me. You will eventually."

The man suddenly broke down into fits of sobbing. Gary pulled him into a hug. Letting the man cry himself dry. Eventually the man finished and leaned back in his seat.

"I don't think I'd never cried like that. This place..." Ralph said.

"It does something, right? It's to help you move on."

"I'm sorry, Gary. I should have done more when you died. Everyone thought it was suspect. I didn't do anything though. I guess I should have known. I can't believe my VP would do this to me, though." Ralph shook his head.

Gary listened to the man's burdens. It took years.

Gary found himself sitting at a Playschool play table. He was drinking imaginary tea. There was a sobbing girl at the table with him.

"Hey, there. Do you want some tea? Your dolly's already got her tea." Gary asked gently.

The girl sniffled and looked up at him. She shifted defensively.

Gary smiled and sipped at his tea. Every hour or so he would refill everyone's cup. He let the girl be. Her name was Ashley, but she preferred Ash. Her life had been slowly trickled to Gary, as if whatever system doled out life stories was making sure not to overwhelm Gary.

"Thank you for taking care of Princess Gloria for me." The girl's voice cut into Gary's musings.

"Oh, of course! I couldn't imagine doing anything else. She's been telling me how thirsty she's been and how good your tea is. She just can't get enough!"

The girls smiled and lapsed back into silence.

After another hour Gary turned to the girl, "Do you know what goes well with tea?" She shook her head in response. "Scones!" He turned to a play set kitchen, which only appeared when he turned towards it. He busied himself pretending to make scones. He set a timer on the oven and sat back down enjoying more tea.

The timer dinged, Gary got up, put on some oven mitts and pulled out a steaming tray of blueberry scones.

"Those look so good. OOOO!" Ash squealed.

Gary smiled in return and put a scone on her plate. He pushed a pad of butter towards her and a little thing of strawberry jam, her favorite.

The table changed to a picnic table under some trees. There was a babbling creek behind them. Gary poured them both some peppermint tea. He made sure Ash saw the sugar cubes.

He sat back and enjoyed his buttered scones and the breeze on his face.

Gary heard sobs from Ash. He glanced over to see a terrified look on her face.

"Please, please, please, don't tell mom and dad that I ate this scone. I didn't earn it. You know. I..." She started to hyper ventilate.

"It's ok. You don't need to earn food any more. You can eat as much as you want."

She gave him a suspicious look.

"I know I need to earn your trust. I'll prove it to you, over time. If you want, you can call me Gary."

"Ok. Gary."

"Looks like Princess Gloria is really enjoying her scone."

Ash looked over to find Gloria covered in scone crumbs and butter smeared on her cheeks. She giggled. Then rushed over with a napkin to clean the face.

"Mom's gonna kill me if she sees this."

"Here, let me." Gary gently took the doll from Ash. He wiped the doll's face and the crumbs and butter vanished. "There, all better."

Ash grabbed the doll hugging her tight.

It took Gary a year to truly earn Ash's trust. To help her feel safe. Only to lose it when he told her the truth of her death. It took a decade for her to finally move to the other side. She was a happy child by that point. Gary had nearly shattered by what her parents had done to her.

"You know, I still can't believe she got away with it." Frank said. "I think it was because she slept with then quickly married that DA. I can't believe she became president after he died."

"That right?"

"Oh yea. Ralph Winston, what a corrupt man. Gary, you were a good man. I regret taking that contract."

"Wait, what contract?"

"The one your wife offered to take you out. She wanted your

business."

"But you almost killed her!"

Frank laughed, "Yea, but she knew you were going to save her. She wasn't dumb, asked me to make it look like an accident and innocent in the whole thing."

Gary clenched his fist, he sighed and let it go. "Well, I guess that makes this part of my job easy. Frank, you're dead. You're not dreaming."

Frank picked up a martini, "I kinda figgerred, since I was talking to a man I killed an all." He took a sip then gestured with the base of the glass. "So, what is all of this then?"

"This. This is where you unburden yourself and then you move on."

"Why?"

"Can't have you haunting decent people back home. So you need to let all of that go."

"This like therapy for dead people or something?"

"You know how people say things like, 'your suffering will lead to good things' or 'God works in mysterious ways' in response to suffering?"

"Yea. So?"

"It's bullshit. I had to tell this young girl she was dead. She had lived a short tortured life. Her mom killed her for 'seducing' her father. The poor girl wasn't even 10 yet. Nothing good came from that suffering. I helped her for something like a decade. Eventually, she was able to put down that suffering. She became a joyful child. One that would have made the world a brighter better place.

"Yes, this is therapy for dead people. It's more than that, though. It's a place where you can become the best version of you. What weren't you allowed to be when you were a kid, Frank?"

"Fuck you. I ain't telling you that."

Gary shrugged and leaned back in his seat. He transformed the seedy run down bar into a school's theater. A young Frank was practicing lines before an audition. His name was called by the Director. Frank was nervous, he took a breath and confidently started into reciting the lines.

He was mid soliloquy when the theater doors banged open. A

large man burst into the theater shouting, "Frank! Get the fuck down from there. No son of mine is gonna be a theater-"

"Sir! You can't barge in here like that! Your son was doing great."

The man dragged Frank from the stage without another word.

They were suddenly in the bar. Frank was seething.

"That wasn't fair." Gary said. "I guess I'm still a little angry about you killing me. Which is fair."

Frank lunged at Gary, throwing a punch at his head. Gary stepped back and let Frank beat on a Gary shaped punching bag.

Eventually Frank wore himself out. He fell to his kneels on the bag's chest. He looked up at Gary and said, "Fuck you Gary. You know what. You were fucking clueless. That wife of yours was running around on you."

Gary nodded sadly, "I know. You know how you can clearly see your life? I can clearly see all my mistakes too. I can see everything. I knew, but refused to acknowledge it."

Gary helped Frank up as he continued, "I've set those burdens down. Though, you've laid new ones on my shoulders. I guess we get to work through these together."

"Great."

"You were very good, you know. You would have made a dashing Macbeth."

"I know. I did some acting after my old man died. I still had the chops for it."

Frank looked Gary up and down, "So, how does all this work. How long are we stuck together."

"As long as it takes."

Neither were surprised that it took years.

"I really did lead quite the life, you know. From nothing, to President. Real rags to riches story. I really need to call my agent to get a movie made. The first act ending with the loss of Gary will be so very moving. Don't you think?"

Gary looked at Sara, "I'm dead at the end of the first act, huh?"

Sara started, spilling her coffee all over her white suit. "Gar-Bear? what are you doing here? how are you here? You're... you're dead."

"So are you, my dear. Do you remember where you were last?"

"I was heading to bed. It'd been a long day. I just submitted a draft of my book. I sat down for my evening coffee."

"Now you're in the Oval Office again. You finished up as president, 5 years ago. Remember?"

"Something was wrong with my coffee. Tasted of almonds. You know I hated the fake flavoring. Give me black coffee."

"Black as your heart?"

"Gary! How could you say that?"

"I've greeted both Ralph and Frank. Your accomplices. I see you also helped pave your way to the Presidency. Husband and Wife President and Vice President. Amazing. I gotta hand it to you."

"I'm proud of myself. I worked hard to get where I did."

"So, you and I have to work through your burdens, before you can move on to the other side. That's going to take a while. You have to come to terms with who you are."

Sara waved a hand. "It'll be no time at all."

Gary spent the next 200 years with Sara.

Gary looked over at Tim.

"I really hate this pub," Tim said. "My friends like to come here though. I don't know why. Maybe it's the cheap drinks? Good people here though."

"Hi Tim. Pleasure meeting you. I'm Gary."

"Surely there are better bars to visit than this hole in the wall."

"Well, for you, Tim. You see, you hated and loved this place so much that you picked here to come first, after you died."

"I'm, I'm dead?"

"Yes. I'm afraid so. You see, I greet the dead. It's my job."

"Who are you then? Fucking Gary? What kind of name is that? You're the Grim Fucking Reaper!"

Gary smiled, "I guess you could look at me that way. No, I'm here to offer you a choice. We can work on unburdening yourself of all your pain and suffering. Or you can replace me. I'm tired. I've been doing this for so long."

"What do you mean? Become death? I am become death, right?"

"Pretty much. Greet the recently deceased and help them through their pain and suffering."

"How does that work?"

"Times different here. Works in circles."

Tim waved to Gary as death walked out the pub door. He scratched his chin, he did help himself a bit ago, didn't he?

What you read next are the many lives Death lives through. The lives he experiences. The lives that he must help the dead move beyond from. Each person, that Tim meets, has lived a difficult life with their own hang ups. Things they must move through. Death isn't just constrained to one single world. Tim transcends worlds and time.

Dominic

He sat up and pivoted to get out of bed. His legs didn't move. They stayed put. He got a nice back crack out of his effort, but the legs had stayed where they were. He glanced down at his atrophied legs, then he looked to the ceiling, tears formed at the edges of his eyes. He groaned.

"It was a dream," the man wailed. "I was running. RUNNGIN! No, no, no, no." dropped his face into his hangs, sobbing.

He felt a shadow fall over him. It was her. She was in the door way. He could feel her disgust radiating towards him. Instead of looking at her, to bear the weight of that withering look, he blindly groped for his wheel chair. He pulled it close and managed to get himself into its confines.

The door way brightened as she left. He felt lopsided in his chair, one arm was higher than the other. He reached under his thin, boney butt and found a book. He pulled it out. The cover read "Dominic's Journal" he opened the first page.

"My therapist said this would help me deal with the trauma of losing functionality of my legs. I'm not sure how. June 7, 2053." Below it were a series of tick marks. They went on for pages. Dominic finally found the end of the hashes. He crossed it, turning it into a five.

He glanced at the top of the page and began tapping groups of fives. 73. Dominic grunted. He tapped his wrist augmentation, "Is today June 7th?"

A disembodied voice replied, "Yes, Dominic, it is June 7th, 2072."

Dominic wrote a giant 20, below the last tick mark and closed the journal, only to open it to the back of the book. There was another set of tick marks. He added another mark. This was a fresh tick with a completed 5 next to it. He glanced at the top of the page reading "Days since a suicidal dream." There were 6 tick marks. Out of the corner of Dominic's eye, he could see a number of pages removed.

"Sir, might I recommend that you write your dream in your journal. That's actually what Dr. Willard suggested you do. You can learn quite a bit from your dreams." The disembodied voice caused Dominic to jump.

"Fuck off."

Dominic wheeled himself to the bathroom to get through his morning routine. Fortunately, the bathroom was designed with his needs in mind. The toilet had a mechanism to slide him over it. There was a lift in front of the sink that locked him in place and let him brush his teeth.

He made his way to the kitchen. She was watching the news. "20 years ago today, Dominic Reyes - "

"Turn that shit off." Dominic cried.

"No, Dom. I'm going to keep watching it." She sounded like she'd be crying. Her voice was thick. She stood, so she could see him over the back of the couch. "I haven't watched it since -"

Dominic cut her off, "Fine, do whatever you want." He tapped his wrist, "Play playlist 4. Increase noise cancellation to maximum."

He could see her lips moving, but couldn't hear what she was saying. He turned to the kitchen and pulled a meal out of the freezer. He tossed it into the convection oven and waited.

He felt himself get hugged from behind and his music abruptly stop. "Dom, they released all the video. It vindicated you. Someone hacked the Global Space Agency and got everything. They just played it live for the first time ever. The GSA was blindsided by it."

Dom felt a kiss on his cheek, "They proved you're the hero I always knew you were. I never doubted."

Dominic's ear piece rang, the caller ID indicating it was GNN. "Dom, you should answer that." She whispered.

The oven dinged. She got the food out for him, poured him

some juice and a mug of coffee while he was struggling to decide if he should answer.

"Hello?" He answered unsure.

"Hello, is this Dominic Reyes?" A professional sounding voice rapidly asked.

"Yes, this is Dominic."

"Great! Viewers, I am here with Dominic Reyes. What reaction do you have to the hacking of the GSA and leak of video evidence that you're a hero?"

"I have none. It's always been my position that I acted in the best interest of Earth. I have not watched any coverage of my actions in the past 20 years and have no idea what you're talking about."

"I'm going to share with you the video now. We're showing it live on air too."

"Good-bye." Dominic ended the connection.

On the news behind Dominic, he heard an echo of his good-bye followed by audio of the event. Dominic buried his face in his hands crying tears of relief. A dam burst. Years of self-hatred and regret flowed through those tears.

His wife, Julia, held him through it all. He reached up and hugged her back. He felt her tears on his cheek. "Dom, you know I've always believed you, right? I have always been here. Now, everyone else will believe you too."

Dominic's food grew cold, untouched, on the table.

I'd Rather Fish, as the World Ends

The sound of the world ending woke him up. Mitch lived in DC, well, the outskirts of DC. You know, one of those suburbs that are within an hour's metro ride to all the government buildings. He was in Maryland, where the cost of housing was a little more reasonable, at least compared to Northern Virginia.

The world ended. DC, it was completely gone. The first explosion woke him. The second, he saw the brilliant light through his lights out curtains - they were blackout curtains. The third one blew out his windows. The curtains were just thick enough to contain most of the glass, just thick enough.

Mitch ran into the bathroom. He jumped into the tub and pulled all the towels over his head that he could. He waited.

While he cowered in his shower, he decided the end of the world was a lot less exciting than it was made out to be in many movies. Mitchel worked for the State department, so he knew he should be trying to log into... something. He was certain there was someone running a meeting right now trying to figure out what to do.

After a quick cry, Mitchel worked up the courage to crawl out of the tub. He smelled smoke. His curtains hung in tatters. His bed was covered in glass.

Mitchel found his slippers next to the bed. After giving them a very vigorous shake, he slipped them on. With his feet more adequately protected, he shuffled to his work bag. He tried to pull out his laptop, only to find his bag shredded and a good size hole in the plastic shell of the laptop.

Mitchel shuffled into his kitchen, which faced away from DC. He grabbed his cell phone and his iPad. Both worked fine. However, there was no internet.

Mitchel walked to his TV, turned it on. The screen stayed black. He glanced about. His shoulders fell, there were no lights on in the house that he could see. Even the coffee maker's light was off.

In the light of the fires, he dressed, putting on some work boots. Steel toed, just in case. He opened the door to his garage. His asshole neighbor's tree had fallen through the roof onto his car.

Mitchel's phone suddenly rang. He jumped. He nearly fumbled his phone. He held the phone to his ear, he could see his hand shaking as he tried to hold it. "Mitch here."

"Mitch, it's Gerry. Can you log into Foggy Bottom?"

"No sir. Glass destroyed my computer, right through the Lenovo logo. I didn't even have phone service for a while there."

"Right. Well, I can't connect to it. We have some servers up somewhere. It's time for us to rendezvous at site B."

Mitchel blew a hard breath, "My car's totaled. Tree fell through the garage."

"Figure something out. Be there in 12 hours. Gerry out."

"12 hours?! Middle of no where Pennsylvania in 12 hours? fuck." Mitchel cried to no one in particular.

Mitchel returned to his house. Mitchel grabbed his coat and shrugged it on, then thought better of it and packed some food and extra clothes. He grabbed his personal laptop and a couple chargers.

He walked outside to see his asshole neighbor gawking at his downed tree. Mitchel walked over to him. Sonny was a much larger man than Mitchel, but Mitchel was tired of this bull shit.

"Sonny, I need your car now. You didn't fucking fix your god damned tree and now, at the END of the FUCKING world, it destroyed my car. Now, I gotta drive for work. State business. I don't have a car. Make this. Right."

Sonny gave him an innocent look, "What do you mean? Make this right. You never offered to pay for an -" Mitchel punched Sonny as hard he could. Sonny collapsed into a heap.

Sohla came running towards Mitchel, "What was that for? Mitch! What's going on?"

Mitchel gestured towards DC, "The city is burning. Foggy Bottom might be gone. I need to meet my team. You have two cars. Give me one for now. Once this is over you'll get it back and I'll get a new car."

She gave him a look. She wasn't stupid. She worked for an agency too. So did Sonny. There was a good chance she'd never see Mitchel again let alone the car.

She glanced at DC, then back to Mitchel. She stormed off into the house. The garage opened minutes later. Their small car was pulling out of the parking space. She got out.

She grimaced as she handed over the keys. "I'm sorry you and Sonny didn't get along. Good luck."

"Thanks Sohla." Mitchel shrugged, "These things happen. Maybe I'll see you at site B or another site."

He hopped in before she could respond and took off. The driving was treacherous. Power lines were down. Cars and trucks were crashed all over the road. As he inched through the traffic, he heard people wailing about blindness.

Mitchel continued. He hoped he could get past Baltimore and Pittsburgh without much problems. He could probably bypass much of Pittsburgh if he went north of it. Baltimore might be harder, he was so close to it.

As Mitchel came closer to the city, he found he had a lot and a little to worry about. Like DC, it was on fire. Like DC, it was mostly a destroyed husk of what it was. However, that meant traffic and cars on the road. People were panicking. The emergency broadcast channel was playing loops of cautions, but not providing any news.

Once Mitchel got far enough away from the large cities, power came back. cell coverage returned. usually the places he cursed for shitty coverage and bad food, had coverage and at least something to eat.

A few hours after being on the road, he stopped at a Sheetz. He got some food and a coffee.

As he filled up a local stopped him, "Is it true?"

"Is what true?" Mitchel asked.

The man pointed at the license plate, "That DC's gone? I heard NYC's gone too." He squinted at Mitchel, "You got a sun burn man? Oh shit, wait, I remember seeing Chernobyl, were you close to the blast?"

Mitchel paused and looked at his hands. They were red. bright red. The gas pump thumped as it stopped filling. "Yea. I uh, I was close. A tree fell on my house from the blast."

"Fuck man, get the hell away from me." The man ran back towards his car.

Mitchel plopped into the car. Sohla's car. She was probably in worse shape than him. Mitchel plugged his phone back in. He dialed a number.

"What is it Mitchel?"

"Ger, I think I have radiation poisoning. Does Site B have detectors?"

"I'll make sure they pull them out. We'll set up different rooms for you and anyone else that's poisoned." There was a pause on the other side, "I'll probably be joining you there. See you soon Mitch."

"Yea, Ger."

Mitchel decided to get some more food. If he was going to be dying soon, he'd at least get another MTO.

By the time Mitchel made it to Boyers, site B, the Iron Mountain. His hair was starting to fall out. He just hoped he'd do some good before he went.

Mitchel parked and staggered his way out of the car. He'd barely made the 12 hour timeline. Traffic was terrible, even with so many people dead. Mitchel was pulled into a side building, away from the rest of the folks. The people unaffected by the bombs.

Blood was dripping from Gerry's nose when he greeted Mitchel. "Yea, I'm getting worse. I had to drive close to Pittsburgh. That second dose may've done me in. Here take these. Might save your life."

Mitchel took the pills. "What's the plan."

Gerry snorted. "No plan to speak of." Gerry sat heavily, coughing. "Shouldn't have snorted."

After his coughing fit passed, he continued, "Well, since I'm basically dead, you're the highest ranking person in the state department. SoS is gone. Internationally, we responded with nukes, too. No one is talking to us. When we tried talking, they blamed us for everything."

Gerry handed Mitchel an envelope, "Here, get caught up."

Apparently, World War III, was like WWI. One small incident set it off. It escalated quickly and beyond anyone's control. Allies were pulled in on every side. Of course, the US had a lot of enemies. We were the biggest, so they decided to neutralize the US first. We responded in kind. Like WWI, everyone is settling back and waiting. Waiting to see what it means to survive after all these major city bombings.

Mitchel put the folder on the table. He just said he was getting something from his car. He left. he went to his brother's cabin in West Virginia. No cell phones. Sure they could find him there, but given everything else going on, why would they bother.

Mitchel's brother Adam found him. He was collapsed along the creek in the back of the property. There were a handful of dying fish in their caught fish pool.

Consequences

She laughed at him. What an absurd thing to say. She laughed and gave him a dismissive wave. His face turned into a storm cloud, which caused her to laugh even harder.

"Listen, dude. Fuck off." She firmly stated. "I don't need to ask your permission to exist."

She turned away before he could respond. She knew it was a risk, but one she needed to take. If she didn't, things would continue to escalate. This was a type of escalation, but she needed to get out. To get away from him. He was one of those dangerous men that claimed to be nice guys, but were women haters. He'd claim to be a victim, but he was the abuser here.

She felt movement behind her. She turned just in time to avoid his grasping hand. Hr bicep mere centimeters from his finger tips. She noticed his T-Shirt was gone, now he was wearing a fine blue suit, with his hair parted down the center, rather than the side.

She noted this as she let her spin throw her fist forward, directly into his right eye. He staggered back, cursing her. He looked up at her, murder in his eyes, as blood poured from his nose.

She found herself striding towards a receptionist in a well lit corporate office's foyer. There was natural like spilling in from the gigantic floor to ceiling glass walls. She could see her looming shadow on the pristine white marble.

"Good morning, I'm here for an interview with Margret McKinney." She greeted the Receptionist.

"Ms. Richardson?" The faceless receptionist replied.

"That's me."

Ms. Richardson was being led into a conference room by a young black woman, Sara. She was wearing some earrings Ms. Richardson had been thinking of buying. They looked great in person like this.

She sat down and made small talk with the woman. Shortly after greeting. He walked in. He had a black eye. His right eye was blackened. The bruising extended down to his nose. There was dried blood on his upper lip.

He gave her an overly warm smile. "Ms. Richardson, such a pleasure to meet you. I've heard so much from Sara", he indicated the young black woman, "about you." He was wearing a Blue Suit. His hair was parted in the center.

She glanced at Margret, "Did he tell you how he got that black eye? He stalked me last night and tried to sexually assault me." She raised her right hand, her knuckles were cut and bruised.

Margret grabbed his arm. They left the room. Sara came in moments later. "It appears we have a VP position opening up soon that we think you're qualified for, bear with us as we get some other folks to interview you."

Ms. Richardson smiled and nodded in response to Sara.

Moments later she walked out with Sara to a different conference room. The man in the blue suit was being man-handled into the back of a police car. As he was pushed into the car, she noticed that his T-Shirt was rumpled and bloody. His jeans torn.

Nikole started out of bed. She grabbed her cell phone. There he was. Bloody. Jeans ripped. She flipped to Linked In. There he was. Blue suited, center part. VP of Marketing.

She took a long shower. She smiled to herself.

She was sitting talking with Susan, waiting for Him to join. Susan was a polite woman from HR, typical type of interviewer. She was to help shepherd her through the interview process.

He finally showed up. 10 minutes late. His eye was noticeably bruised. He had a scrape on his face. She glanced down at her knuckles.

"It was you." Nikole turned to Susan, "Susan, do you know why he has that bruise on his face?"

Bloody murder flashed on his face. But she'd seen it before. She smiled at him as she explained to Susan what happened.

21

Catch and Release

Eric put down the rod. The fish just weren't biting. Maybe he was just missing the nibbles. He reached down to grab the rod again, something whistled over his head. He dropped down to the ground and looked towards where the thing would have gone. There was an arrow quivering in a moss covered partially submerged tree.

He heard some scattering of conversation. Obviously whoever had shot at him wasn't too concerned about him retaliating or almost being hit. As he sorted out what to do, his rod still in his hand, an arrow cut through some moss and skittered off a stone a few inches from his face.

Eric glanced up and noticed the rod was sticking straight up in the air. He cursed silently to himself. As he was cursing, he heard similar commotion coming from the same spot as the first arrow. The second arrow suddenly retracted. Eric started. He hadn't even seen the cabling on the arrow. Did they not have more arrows?

Eric found something that he could secure the fishing rod standing up along the bank, so we could figure out what was going on.

As he was crawling north, along the river, parallel to where the archers were, he heard an arrow thunk into a log. The log he'd placed to hold the rod upright. He got up into a crouch to move more quickly. His footsteps were hidden over the crashing and dragging noise coming from the log.

Eric stopped when the log noises seemed to stop. Whoever was pulling on that arrow was strong, or the arrow had released from the log. He lowered himself, trying to hide himself in the tall grass along the bank.

His hand touched a rock. He silently pulled it out of the ground. He rotated and threw the rock south, past where his rod was still laying. It bounced off the riverbank and splashed loudly into the water.

Eric heard more excited noises to his immediate west. The noises, didn't sound like any language he'd heard. Not that he was a linguist or anything like that. He could barely speak English.

The bow raised, he was only 15 feet away from the archers. They seemed to have moved closer to the fishing rod. He heard the twang of the bow. Then hear a hiss as the line unreeled. The arrow splashed into the water. The archer began to reel the line back along with the arrow. It sounded like it was dragging something.

Eric took advantage of the noise. He started to walk towards the archers. He had firm branch in one hand and his phone in the other. He was going to flash them and whack them, then run like hell out of there.

The archers make a screeching noise as he got closer. He heard one of the archers run away from the other. Eric took his chance. He dashed forward snapping a picture, the flash blinded his target. He swung, before he really even saw who he was swinging at.

There was a meaty thunk and a crunch. Eric reached for the bow, to take away the weapon when he processed what he had hit. It was a fish. A fish. It was a fish. It was a trout. A fish was shooting at people.

It was a 6 foot tall fish. It had a contraption over the gills and over it's mouth. It was a fish.

It was flopping on the ground. He'd broken something near the top of its mouth. Water was shooting everywhere.

Eric staggered back. He tripped over a man. There were three men stuck together in a giant hook. All three pierced through in about the same spot back through to the chest. All three were gasping for breath. They weren't dead, yet, but they definitely were dying.

Eric ran, then. He reached the road and called 911. When the cops showed up, he took them to the site. There was blood everywhere. The three men had been released. There was no sign of the archers. One of them died. The other two managed to survive.

Eric never did go fishing again.

Out of Time

Emily woke with a start. She shouldn't have been sleeping. She glanced about. No one was looking her way. Though, none of the other students looked familiar. She scratched her neck. There was an odd bump there.

The professor wasn't in class yet. She glanced at the time. 3:45. She pulled out her phone. It was still 3:45. She tapped in her passcode and pulled up her calendar. It was Thursday. She didn't have any afternoon classes.

"Hey, was I here when you came in?" the girl in front of her jumped.

"Where the fuck did you come from?" She cried. She held her chest as she started to panic. "You weren't here when I came in. I didn't hear you sit behind me."

"Yo. What the fuck? Who are you?" came an androgynous voice behind her.

Emily spun, "Hi, I'm Emily. I have no idea how long I've been sleeping here. Do you?"

"No. You, uh, literally appeared in front of me when you spoke with Sally. I was watching Sally play with her hair when you asked her your question." They blushed when they said that.

Sally blushed in response. Emily stood, loudly pushing her desk to the side. A guy three rows over shrieked. She staggered back, running into another chair, knocking into another student.

"What are you doing throwing your desk into me? Wait. Emily? Emily Robiniski? You were in my Calc 1 class like 2 years ago.

You disappeared in the middle of a final."

Emily shuddered, pulling her jacket tighter on herself. She looked at her phone again, "Wait, it's 2021?" She dropped her phone and quickly followed it to the floor. She stuttered, "No, no, it can't be." She looked at the guy she pushed her desk into. "You, we were going to study abroad in Paris together, weren't we?"

"I did, well, it was cut short in 2020, because of the pandemic, but you didn't go. You were missing. Your family freaked out. Where did you come from?"

Emily looked down at herself, "I, I," she cleared her throat, "I dozed during the Calc final and woke up here." She grabbed her coat from the back of her chair, but there was no coat to grab.

She sprinted out of the class room. She ran into someone as she rounded the corner. She fell to the ground sobbing. She felt a huge weight fall on her shoulders.

"Miss, are you alright?" A familiar voice asked.

"I'm, I'm alright. I don't know what's happening." She looked up at the person she ran into. She gasped, "Jeremy? I'm so glad to see you." She threw herself onto him. Giving him a tight hug.

"Miss, I don't know who you are." He said politely. He gently pulled her off of him. He gasped as he got a good look at her face. "Emily? My god? Where have you been? I missed you so much. Your parents were a mess."

He staggered back. "Your parents." He could look at her. He wiped at tears in his eyes.

"What about my parents? One minute I was in a Calc final the next I'm waking up in a classroom with no idea what'd happened. Jimmy, mentioned a pandemic, that it's 2021. What's going on Jeremy?" Emily cried.

"We better get you to a hospital. Hold on a second. I'll text your sister. She needs to meet us there. Do have a mask?"

"A mask? Like a costume mask?" She asked confused.

He stared back, "You've no idea what I'm talking about, do you? Covid? the Pandemic. 600,000 dead in the US. Ring a bell?"

"You're joking right? I remember watching some movies about a plague. That'd never happen here though. Sweetheart, just tell me what's going on."

He broke down into tears. "Emily, we thought you ran off somewhere. You've been gone since mid December 2019, it's May of 2021. Everyone assumed you were gone. Then with Covid, we just assumed you were dead. There was so much pain and loss. Then your parents." He trailed off. Before he continued, "After they passed away, I moved in with your sister. We've been a couple for six months now. We thought you were gone. Oh god. How are you back?"

"Sarah, you and Sarah? You hated her. She couldn't stand you. What are you going on about? Mom and Dad can't be dead. I just talked with them." Emily's eyes were wide, she was shaking her head. She was hoping this was all a dream.

Jeremy gave her a pained look. "Come on. Let's go." He glanced at his phone. "Your sister's outside."

The pair staggered outside, both in a daze. A relatively new BMW stood waiting outside for them. Sarah popped out and ran to Jeremy.

After a quick kiss she asked, "What's this madness about Emmy?"

Jeremy's eyes were mostly unfocused as he gestured towards Emily. Sarah looked at the woman next to him. Emily's mouth hung open. Her eyes were filling with tears. Her face began to shatter into heart break.

"Emmy? Emmy! EMILY?! Is that really you?" Sarah cried. She wrapped her older sister in a firm hug. A rib creaking hug. Emily didn't return the hug.

As soon as Sarah broke the hug, Emily collapsed into herself. She sat down on the curb, she began to sob. "You and Jeremy, how long?"

Sarah gasped, bringing her hand to her mouth, "Oh my god. We thought you were dead. It's been about, November or so. We were just so alone. First his dad, then our parents. It was just, just too much to bear."

Emily moaned, she started to cry hard. Her full body started to shake. "What" *gasp,* "year" *sniff,* "is it?" Emily finished with a terrified look.

Sarah looked at Jeremy. He looked exhausted, he responded to Sarah, "You need to tell her the truth."

She looked back at her sister, "It's May of 2021. You've been missing almost a year and a half. With all the other loss of the year. We were some of the first to grieve. 2020 was a brutal year."

Sarah sank to her knees, "Where were you?" her voice was harder and angrier than she meant.

Emily shook her head, "Nowhere. I don't know. I don't know. I don't know." She broke down sobbing.

Jeremy rubbed his face, "Let's get her to the E.R. and go from there. We can at least get her a vaccine while we're there, if nothing else."

The Emergency Department was full of sick and injured people. Many wore paper masks, one or two angry people left the hospital before really entering. They had been refused for endangering others.

Emily stared about, her mask sitting on her face as if she'd never worn a mask. Her eyes were large and owl like. Taking in everything, rarely blinking, and with dilated pupils.

Sarah went with Emily as she was taken back by the nurse.

"So, tell me about what's going on with your memory?" the nurse politely asked.

"No, it's not a memory thing. I was literally in a Calc final. I felt myself start awake and I was in a strange class room. The students were terrified when I showed up." Emily said, repeating exactly what she'd said to the admitting clerk.

Sarah quickly interjected, "She's been missing for a year and a half. She disappeared from that final. We thought she was kidnapped. Or maybe died by suicide. She has a 'cold' missing persons case. We wanted to get her checked to make sure she was alright given what's happening out in the world."

The nurse nodded, "I'll take her vitals and get some blood drawn. We'll see if you've been drugged or anything. Ok?"

Emily nodded, doubtfully.

The nurse professionally wrapped a blood pressure cuff around Emily's left arm and turned on the automatic pressure measurement machine. The nurse was typing in a chart when she heard one of the women gasp. She quickly turned her head when the cuff suddenly hit the floor.

The nurse turned to find the chair empty. Sarah was staring

in horror at the chair. Sarah began to scream.

29

MountainFall

Sam looked out the window. The mountain was on fire. The entire face of the mountain was ablaze. He was over 30 miles away but he could still see the smoke. He could smell the smoke. The worst part was that the trees would burn relatively quickly, the bigger problem was the coal fire burning under the mountain.

A coal fire started in the mine 30 miles from the mountain about 50 years ago. It wasn't a mine in the town Sam was in, but the next one over. It killed the mine, sent the whole area into a recession. Most of the towns in the area never recovered. Sam had been watching this fire for years.

Sam was a mine drone technician, well, he was more than that, but that's easiest to say. The state government had required Morrison Mining Inc, MMI, to setup a team to track all their coal fires. They had a few. This one was the largest. The vein of coal had forked. Not once or twice, but dozens of times. They had planned on doing some mountain top mining, just cutting down the entire mountaintop to get to this coal, but they had waited too long.

Sam picked up his mug. His coffee was hot, he liked the dark roast. The darker the better. That bitterness and smokiness really woke him up. He couldn't handle the caffeine of the lighter roasted stuff. This woke him up better than that though. It tasted like a punch to the face. He loved it. Felt invigorated by the sharpness of it.

As he sipped he noticed his windows vibrate. He saw a water helicopter flying overhead, heading towards the fire. Sam shook his head. The fire didn't start because of anything on the surface. The ground was so hot, it caught the trees above it on fire. There'd been a long drought and that dried out the trees, but the coal fire was raging below.

Sam took another sip and grabbed his laptop. He fired it up. It was an older machine, so it took a while to boot. It gave him time to watch the water spill from the back of the helicopter, flash into steam as the helicopter wheeled away. Others followed it.

Sam quickly logged into his Linux machine. He pulled up his drone control program. He managed the swarm. They were a semi-autonomous smart drone system. The swarm was made of microdrones. These created a mesh network to share information across the drone network and to maximize distance covered along multiple forks at once.

Sam pulled on his goggles. He had used the drones to build a 3D map of the coal veins as they were burning. Well, after they had burnt. He had a leading edge of drones that were essentially fireproof. Other drones followed behind to extend the network and to map in more detail the results of the fire.

He was pretty proud of himself. He'd modified the code and the drones themselves to build this network. MMI had turned his drones into a consultancy and made even more money off of these disasters.

Sam fumbled for his coffee. He liked holding it while he was in VR, it helped ground him in reality. It kept him from feeling stuck in these tiny crawl ways. He had a suit that gave him for of an idea of the temperature in there, but figured that the warmth of his coffee would make him feel both there and far from it.

He checked the leading edge of the drones. The heatproof ones. They converted a lot of that heat into power, power and RF. That RF was how they built the mesh networks. One of his team members had figured out how to harvest RF from the air, not a ton, but enough to keep the drones powered and moving. It was a useful system.

Sam sat up. He had noticed something. He did a quick survey. He threw off his goggles and quickly wrote up a positioning script. The script looked at the relative rates of specific vein fires and the directions they were heading. He was concerned a number of them were all leading to the same place.

While the server was crunching the data, there was no way his ancient laptop could manage all that data, he pulled back on his VR goggles and switched his view to one of the drones already in that location.

He didn't understand what he was seeing. The camera's view was normally constrained and tightly focused ahead of the drone. The fire wasn't a single pinpoint. It was a wall. It was raging above and below the drone.

He switched to a trailing drone with a larger camera. Specifically designed to map large pockets of burned out coal. The space was huge. No wonder the mountain was on fire. There was a huge pile of coal burning there.

He got a message from the server indicating the mapping was complete. Sam had the server run it again. The results made no sense. The second run had the same results. He checked his code. He rewrote part of it using different equations. Similar results, to the point that there was no appreciable difference.

Sam keyed his messaging app, he Direct Messaged Ivan: Hey, could you check out these results. I've never seen anything like it. Here's the branch.

Ivan responded almost immediately: Sure dude! hope you're having a good morning. I'm getting ready to call it a night soon. Hopefully this is quick.

Sam: It's going to be a long day for me, I think. Copters already dumping water on :fire:

Ivan: :grimacing: code looks good. trying to map out where the veins are going. Running

Sam: Ok. let me know when you get the results.

Ivan: what the actual fuck. dude. You need to report this. Get people off that mountain.

Sam: Fuck. Same results then. Thanks man. Good night.

Sam DM'd his boss, Dr. Morrrison: Dr. M You got a minute to talk? Urgent. need to TALK

The system turned into a call. Dr. M appeared in front of Sam.

"What's up Sam?" Dr. M asked tersely.

"Let me share this projection with you." Sam pulled up the video rendering of the projection.

"Who else has seen this?" Dr. M asked.

"Ivan, from the Russia office." Sam replied.

Dr. M nodded, "Call FEMA. Good luck."

Sam ended the call. He quickly pulled up the regional head of FEMA on his phone. He pulled off his VR goggles as he called.

"Hi Sam, what can I do for you?" came a tense voice.

"Get everyone off the mountain Tressie. It's going to collapse." Sam replied.

"What do you mean it's going to collapse?" Tressie angerly replied.

"Tressie, we have about 45 minutes until a massive pocket of coal is burnt through. It will cause a void and the bulk of the mountain will collapse. We should evacuate at least a 30-50 mile radius. I have no idea what sort of earthquakes will be unleashed." Sam shouted.

Tressie coughed, "Don't yell. Send me the data."

Sam had been updating the video in the background. The predicted collapse time line had shrunk to 20 minutes. Sam sent it to her.

Sam stared out the window at the mountain. Willing the fire to stop. Instead, the smoke increased in intensity. "Did you get it?"

Tressie abruptly hung up on him.

Sam shook his head and decided to take care of himself. So he grabbed some food, water, and packed a bag. As he packed the evacuation announcement was sent to his cell phone. He could hear the tornado warning start to wail. Sam grabbed his computer, a charger and tossed the bag over his shoulder. He poured coffee into a thermos and sprinted to his car.

He was turning on to a major thorough way, with the mountain in his rear view mirror, when he saw the top of the mountain disappear.

Seconds later, a shockwave tore through the small town.

Sam's car left the ground, it was thrown forward. He landed roughly, his head bouncing against the ceiling. His car screamed in protest. Lights flashed across the dash. His heads-up-display told him to slow down to avoid leaving the ground over bumps.

A second shock was was coming. Sam could see it in his rear view mirror. There was a massive fast moving cloud. He floored it before he could see any more details.

His phone range. It flashed up as Tressie - FMEA. He pushed the answer button, "Tressie, I hope you're on the road!"

"You lying bastard! You said we had 45 minutes." She cried. Their connection cut. His HUD saying call lost. It'd been years since he'd seen that.

Sam called to the car, "Call Dr. M."

The car responded, "There is no cellular networks in the available, would you like to make your call using the satellite service?"

"YES!" Sam cried.

The car's speakers started to ring. "Sam, what's happening?" Dr. M. briskly asked.

"It collapsed already. I sent Tressie the information." Sam saw a shadow out of the rear view mirror, "Oh, fuck. I might lose you here. I hope that isn't pyroclastic."

Sam's car got hot. He ducked down he heard things bash into the rear window. He heard tinking off the roof. it sounded as if he was in a hail storm.

Sam had hoped being 30 miles away would have been far enough. It didn't seem like that was the case. He kept driving, even though he couldn't see the road.

Dr. M. Called to Sam, "Tell me what's happening!"

Sam's car slammed into something moments later.

Sam woke up some time later. He's front windshield was shattered. Tree branches were mere inches from his face. There was something jutting through the passenger's seat. He glanced into the back seat. Then looked up, it looked like part of a house had landed in the back seat.

He slowly pulled himself out of his car. He wasn't sure how he was alive. He should have been dead. He grabbed his bag from the passenger floor. Somehow it seemed to have survived.

Everything was covered in a mix of dust and rocks. Sam pulled his shirt over his nose, hoping to protect himself from the worst of the particles in the air.

He noticed a number of fires, down the street it looked like three houses were on fire. Two cars, electric from the look of the fire, were melting a hole in the ground.

Sam opened his bag. His food looked like it was ok. He'd have at least a meal or two as he tried to walk out of town.

He pulled his phone from his pocket. He switched to satellite mode. He dialed Dr. M.

"My boy! You're alive. Oh, thank god." came an almost immediate response. Despite everything, Sam still grimaced at being called "boy". "I'd been on the line when you crashed. I thought it was over for you."

"Yea. I'm not really sure how I'm alive. This is my car." He took a picture and sent it to Dr. M. "I'm going to head to some place that might have power and water and communication stuff."

"Our satellites are showing a 60 mile radius of destruction. Conserve your battery. I'm sending you coordinates. We'll send a helicopter and pick you up."

"Thank you sir. See you soon." Sam ended the call. He looked around at the devastation. He shook his head and started to sob as he walked.

Davi the Great Sorceress

She strode to her mount. McKay, a young unicorn mare, looked exhausted. They had ridden long and hard to get as far as they had, the poor unicorn would find no rest this night.

Luna, her light gray familiar, looked at her with luminous eyes. She was nestled in a saddle bag. She looked tired even though she could easily rest.

Davi wiped the fatigue from her eyes and pulled herself up onto McKay. She shook her dark hair out of her eyes and looked up the mountain. She could make out the smoke from mountainside homes. The homes in Santfem. Her stomach growled.

"I could really go for some of Mother's chili right about now. Warm me from this frigid cold." she muttered to herself.

Davi kicked McKay into a canter. She prayed that McKay would survive and forgive her for this abuse. It wasn't fair to the unicorn. Davi patted the mare to show her appreciation. She only got a snort in return.

Davi sighed and continued their ascent. An hour later they had arrived at the outlying pueblos surrounding Santfem. Their warriors were out, watching the street for signs of the invaders. The roads were filled with their spies, after all.

They simply waved as Davi raced by. They knew she was coming and the best warriors can feel the movements of animals and unicorns have a distinct feeling.

Another hour passed and Davi arrived at the gates of Santfem. McKay was nearly dead beneath her. She could feel the unicorn trembling. McKay's breath came ragged. Fortunately, Davi could go on alone without her noble friend.

"Ho! Gateman, open and let me in," Davi cried.

"We have orders to allow no one through. The settlers are on their way," bellowed a shaky voice.

"It is I, Davi, the great sorceress, come with glad tidings for the chief."

Without a response, the gate shuddered open. Davi swiftly entered the city. She hopped down from McKay. The mare crumpled to her knees heaving deep breaths. Davi waved her hands and the unicorn began to snore.

Davi turned to the guard, "Give me a horse. McKay needs to rest."

The man grunted and called to a young stablehand to brought a horse to Davi. As she mounted, Luna jumped up in front of the saddlehorn, ensuring she wouldn't be left behind.

Davi tore through the city, leaving a wake of chaos and confusion behind her. She laughed maniacally. She swiftly arrived at the cheif's longhouse.

The doors opened before she could even knock. A voice calling as soon as they opened, "Oh! it's the great Davi! I hope you come bearing good news."

Davi smiled, "I do, great chieftain." Her smile turned evil as she unleashed arms of darkness. Each arm latched onto a person in the hall. Their hands clawed uselessly at the smokey-blackness wrapped tight around their throats.

"My news," She continued as she stalked forward, "is that the invaders will not need a puppet ruler, as they are destroyed."

The chieftain broke into a sweat, "Guards! come quick. Davi, she's gone mad!"

Davi smirked and waved her hands. The chieftain was bound to a chair. He began babbling. Begging for his life. No help materialized.

"I destroyed the Spaniards. They will not be coming. There will be no invaders. Your time is passed."

She turned and looked at her cat. "Luna, he's yours."

The small gray cat grew larger with every step she took. Davi turned her back on the chief. She laughed. "It is now my time."

Mountain Goddess

She struck a pose as she thrust the head towards the sun. The head had been severed recently enough that blood still emptied out of the neck wound. That and she had wrapped it so the blood would stay in the head. The blood dripping added a lot to the effect.

A cry came from the sky. She had been expecting this. She had killed one of their own after all. She threw the head off the mountain top. It quickly tumbled out of sight. A flame burst from where the head might have been. A small explosion followed. She pulled off her gloves and dropped them in the bloody mud next to her mountain bike.

She knew they'd follow her soon. The cursed "gods." She threw her head back and chortled. She was a warrior, she feared no pretender god. They would all end up like what's his name down there.

She spun her bike around and began the steep decent to the valley floor below. She couldn't help notice the sky began to turn a deep red. It wasn't passed mid-afternoon.

She glanced over her shoulder as she pedaled, gathering speed. The sun looked like it was pouring down into the valley. The top half of the sun was already a bright blackness. It stood out in the blood red of the sky.

"You know, Solinea, I am Duarnne and I do not fear you." She, Duarnne, cried. "I will meet you in the valley. I will send you back to whatever hell that spawned you."

Duarnne adjusted a small pump on her bike's frame and began to hurtle down the mountain side. The dying sun cast long shadows on the path. The descent was treacherous with a sky full of sunlight. Now, it was deadly. Duarnne cared not. She grinned as she pedaled faster. Her purple bike deftly handled the worst of the rocks.

Soon, a menacing orange glow greeted her from the bottom of the trail. Even though she had miles before the trail bottomed out, she could see the warm flickering flames.

Solinea, the usurper. The head of this new pantheon. Malloten, the bloody head, had been her consort. He tried to claim the mountains. He had said, "I claim these peaks, as they reach up to touch you, to be closest to you."

These mountains weren't claimable. These mountains were Duarnne's. Malloten refused to admit that.

Purple Rain kicked rocks out from under Duarnne. She heard a few ricochet off near by trees. She was getting closer. Already below the tree line. She switched gears and pedaled harder.

Duarnne found herself swinging passed the valley on a switchback. It was aglow with fire and Solinea's snake. It was difficult to discern where one started and the other ended. The fire obscured the eerie sky, the red and black of the sun. Instead, there was nothing but smoke. Cowards hide behind smoke. Solinea was afraid of Duarnne.

As Duarnne rode closer she began to map her attack vector. There was an arch between Mt. Humor and Mt. Sorrow, Duarnne could launch from there. The snake was coiled around a massive piece of Humor. It had sheared off a millenia ago. The wind had shaped it. It was vaguely head shaped.

Duarnne smirked, she imagined the dumb snake was trying to will the head to turn into her dead lover. Gods do have a lot of power, but they've never had the power to revive one of their own and certainly not a poseur like Solinea.

The path was getting dark, Duarnne glanced up at the sun, it was nearly obsidian. The valley was glowing as bright as the afternoon sun. Duarnne's smirk turned into a wild laugh. Wild and free like a mustang. Like Purple Rain. She could feel the joy from the bike. As if it was joining in with her laugh. Rocks shot out from the bike tires almost in time with her chortle.

Duarnne rounded a curve and there it was, the land bridge arch. It was massive, wide enough for a small village. It was empty though. Fire raged up both sides of the arch, casting strange shadows as the light fought itself.

She threw herself into pedaling. She was going 50 miles an hour, 60, 70, 80. The bridge was there. She glanced down, saw the snake. She judged where the head would be, she'd only have one shot.

She judged her jump well. Solinea moved into her line of attack. Snake's head swung to see what would move into the fire.

Duarnne pulled her bike pump from under her cross bar. She flung her arm down extending the pump. When she brought her arm back up, the pump was a gleaming lance. Duarnne set it in her left pedal, where she had more control and thrust it through the beast's eye.

The snake reared its head, trying to catch Duarnne. She flicked her wheels up to meet the maw, tires caught grip on the scales of Solinea's upper lip.

Duarnne swung the lance's butt forward, scrambling whatever counted for the snake's brain. She felt the opposite eye pop. As Purple Rain naturally pulled her away from the snake's head, Duarnne turned the lance into a giant barbed arrowhead.

She guided Purple Rain rain down the back of the snake, letting her momentum pull the vicious weapon out of the eye socket. Gore and brains followed behind her. Once the weapon fell to the snake's body, she turned it into a razor sharp scythe and let it drag behind her.

Duarnne could feel Purple Rain suffering beneath her. The wheels were catching fire.

Duarnne returned the pump to the frame and pedaled harder and faster than she'd ever pedaled before. The snake thrashed and rolled beneath Purple Rain in an attempt to crush Duarnne or perhaps they were just death throes. Duarnne couldn't tell.

At long last, Duarnne found a safe place to jump from the snakes back. A small cloud of steam indicated a stream. She jumped, landing roughly. The suspension was rock hard. The oil had nearly boiled out.

Duarnne came to a stop and looked back at her handiwork.

The snake had crushed the head shaped rock. The flames were guttering, leaving only the forest ablaze in their wake. That would end soon, as a storm was fast approaching.

Duarnne staggered suddenly. A mind numbing crack pierced the sky. Despite the noise, she glanced sunward. The obsidian shield was shattered. The remains were cast off the sun and smashed upon the snake's corpse.

Duarnne stroked her bike. The tires returned to normal. The suspension sighed in relief.

Duarnne rode back to the arch to look at the stones that crashed upon Solinea. They were shaped in a rough amphitheater shape. The story of her battles were etched into the stones at the top. As she was admiring it, she glanced over, Finn was standing there, Solinea's father, the god of the sun.

"I grant you the title of goddess of the Mountains." Finn boomed.

Duarnne snorted, she grabbed her pump and pointed the sword at his throat. "Two things. You can't give me what I took for myself. You're lucky I like surfing, otherwise I'd have your job."

Finn staggered back. He tried to raise himself up to tower over her, but some how, he just became smaller and smaller.

"Fucking mediocre men." Duarnne scoffed. She turned and wheeled Purple Rain towards the coast. A surfboard appeared on her back.

Trials of Meditation

Robert sat in his favorite chair. This was the chair he sat in every morning for his routine. He just finished his breakfast and was settling in for his meditation. His coffee was still too hot, so he liked to spend about 10 or so minute meditating to cool the coffee enough to drink.

He used an app for his meditation. Despite the criticism of these sorts apps, Robert really enjoyed this. Sure, they could be abused by companies to "boost" productivity or to make a workforce more pliable. However, Robert had really found them to help with his daily anxiety. Anxiety that had been crippling and prevented him from engaging in life, at all.

As he settled in, he smelled his coffee, one of his favorite blends. Holler Mountain, not too dark, with some subtle flavoring that shifted depending on the temperature of the coffee. He'd even found that different flavors would appear if he reheated the coffee.

Robert smiled and leaned back into his chair. It was slightly over stuffed, so the huge arms of the chair almost crowded him. It made him feel very secure. Almost as if his chair was hugging him. The whole setup grounded him and let Robert feel the chair on all sides. The coffee let him smell the world around him. With the windows open he could hear the chirping of the birds.

Robert started his app. The soothing voice suggested he take some deep breaths. He breathed in deeply, smelling his coffee. He felt very connected to his body and to the world about him.

After closing his eyes, he could see where his body was touching the chair. He could feel how it hugged him. He felt his butt was lower than his knees and the cushion was less compressed farther up his thighs.

The hardwood was cool beneath his feet. His hands were warm on his belly and thighs. His began his scan of his body. He was sore from his long bike ride yesterday. He could really feel it in his neck and upper shoulders. His upper back was tight as well. He took a few breaths as he moved down his body, trying to relax.

As he got to his abdomen, he could feel some tension from his dinner last night. He relaxed and felt a fart squeeze through. Robert felt lighter and looser. These scans always seemed to relax his intestines and helped him stay regular.

After finishing up his scan he followed his breath and started to feel where he was breathing. This was always his favorite part. counting his breaths. It really helped him feel his body. Feel how things were working.

The app told him to move into a visualization. Robert's breathing caught. He started to panic. The app told him it was OK if he couldn't visualize the spark of sunlight, that it's important to just keep trying. The efforts is what's important.

Robert imagined the spark. The light on his chest. He saw it expand.

He imagined looking around. Instead of seeing himself in his home, with the well kept overstuffed chair. He was in a long dark hallway. The only light came from his chest. The darkness was oppressive. He could feel the darkness stretching out for him. The horrors in this hallway were overwhelming.

Robert tried to expand the light. He imagined the light was covering his entire body. That it filled him with its warmth, it's lightness, it's brightness.

Robert tried to let the image go, but only the light started to go. The hallway remained. He panicked, the light dimmed. In it's place, darkness swiftly followed, like a squid's ink.

Robert listened to the app, it seemed to be looping now. Telling him to visualize the spark on his chest. It'd always been there. This light, it'd always been a part of him. He's lighting up the world with this spark.

Robert began to image the spark turning into a sphere and filling him. As he did the tendrils of darkness retracted, pulling back to just beyond the light. He imagined the light growing larger, staying light and bright. The warmth kept the frigid air away from him. He could no longer see his breath.

Robert stood, he glanced down, the overstuffed chair was returning to its former glory. He could see the light filling in the sunken cushion, pushing stuffing back into holes and placing leather seamlessly over holes. Robert smiled. He really did love this chair.

He picked up his still warm coffee from the end table, enjoying the smell of his coffee. The warmth of the coffee made the warmth of the light easier to feel. Easier to see. Easier to impose upon the hallway.

Armed with his coffee, Robert pushed forward, filling the hallway ahead of him and behind him with more and more light. He saw doors with cracked and peeling paint, dramatically fixing themselves as he walked by with his light. He could smell the fresh paint. The paint quickly dried, staying fresh and clean.

He opened the closest of the doors. He recognized it as his childhood bedroom. It even had the cross-stitched "Robert's Room" hanging in the center of the door. Robert pushed open the door. The darkness lunged at him. The light in front of him began to fade. He could feel the darkness pressing in from his right side, farther down the hallway.

He tried to remain firm. Tried to image more light, but tendrils burst through the warmth. Their touch was icy cold. They left a freezing hot hand print on his cheek.

He tried to image the light. The warmth. The cold was so intense. He felt so alone.

He heard a voice mockingly saying, "I'll give you something to cry about, you little shit."

Robert glanced to his hand. His coffee was there. He breathed it in. He took steadying breaths. He counted his breaths. Took a sip of coffee. The nutty flavors coated his tongue.

He looked at the spark on his chest. He could hear it saying, "You can be anything."

The darkness coalesced into his mother. He recognized that she was small, scared, unable to cope with the world around her. She lashed out at Robert.

He took a deep breath and imagined a world where she was happy. He struggled. He had only ever wished for her to leave him alone. For her to leave him with a friend. For her to just cease to be. Her happiness, made Robert's spark and light grow. Robert smiled. If he could imaging her being happy, then imagining anyone happy or covered his in light was an easy thing.

He took a few deep breaths. He looked at the happy version of his mother. He shook his head, he'd never seen her look like this. He didn't know if it was even possible.

The image began to crumble. Claws of darkness burst out of her mouth. The happy mother's head wrenched and split. Light spilled out where blood would have poured. The darkness tore off the body of Happy Mother like a molting snake.

Robert shuddered.

The App told him to let the image go. To come back to his body.

Robert tried. he tried to image he was back in the overstuffed chair.

The smell of coffee.

The sound of the birds.

He heard her voice, "That's right boy. Run, run like you always do. I'll be here. Waiting."

Robert opened his eyes. He was back in his favorite chair. Sweating. He took a sip of his coffee. He smiled, just the perfect temperature.

Is that you, Death?

I woke up and found Death's grinning face peering down at me. The face pulled back, allowing me to focus on the rest of the Death's being.

Death cocked its head at me. Then Death glanced about, scratching the top of Death's head.

I realized then that Death wasn't wearing the traditional garb I'd seen Death portrayed in. Death was wearing, what I could only describe as booty shorts. On the top Death was wearing an oversized purple hoodie, that had some characters that I'd never seen before, I'm assuming they were supposed to be letters or something.

Death shrugged, leaned back down towards me. I flinched as Death reached out to pat my cheek. Death spoke then, "Take care of that body, yea? You'll miss it when it's gone." Death's voice was not a deep graveling grating voice like I was expecting. Instead it was a sweet sing songy sound. I was mesmerized.

Death stood then, waved and turned, almost as if Death was flipping some nonexistent hair. Then Death sauntered off. I still do not know how those shorts stayed on.

I took a minute to catch my breath. It's not every day you stare Death in the eye and Death shrugs. I laughed then. Death shrugged. Didn't take my life, but SHRUGGED!

My joy was short lived though. A scream shattered any semblance of relief I may had felt. I looked about, expecting some horror to be unfolding in front of me. Instead it was a smaller Death staring and pointing a bony hand at me. That Death was pulling on the sleeve of a very large Death. That Death was easily 6'5" which towered over my 5'10. I glanced about to see what was behind me. There was nothing but more of the hill I had reclined upon.

The small Death was screaming at me.

"Skinjob!" The large Death boomed at me. This Death did sound very much like I was expecting. Deep grating voice, I've heard rock slides that were gentler.

"Daddy! Why does it have skin?!" The child Death cried.

At this time, I pondered if, in fact, Death was multitudes or if I'd stumbled upon a skeletal land. Perhaps this was a type of afterlife?

"I'm sorry you had to see this," it was difficult to separate words in the tumble of stones. "This, is a skinjob. They are forbidden in our land. I'll deal with it."

"What a minute! Deal with it? Deal with me? What are you going on about?" I cried.

The child skeleton shrieked. I jumped. I did not expect that noise. The child followed this with a question, "How can it talk?! It's got all that meat in the way. It sounds so disgusting."

"I know, dear. Let me call the Skinners. They will know what to do." Boulders bounding broken mountainsides sounded gentler than that massive Skeleton. It thrust a hand towards me, "If you make a move towards my child, I will disembody you myself." It sounded like glaciers baring down on me. I curled into a ball. There was nothing else to do.

He pulled out, what looked like, a small phone. I peaked over my arm to see how he used it. I could see him tapping at the screen, but it never looked like the bone actually touched anything. It was fascinating. Almost as if there was a body, there, but not really there!

As he was dialing, I sprang to my feet. I pivoted away from the pair and sprinted around the hill, away from them. As far from them as I could.

I heard a barrel of rocks explain to his child that the Skinners would get me. I certainly hoped not.

My European ancestors may have been brutal practitioners of scalping, but they never liked it. They needed to pay the bills, you understand. I certainly hoped the Skinners had neither bills nor enjoyed - I shuddered, unable to complete the thought.

Why wasn't that first Skeletal figure that saw me afraid of me.

Why only this pair?

There were more questions than I could answer with the information at hand. Especially, when I was out of breath. This was a steep hill. Why did I end up on this steep hill. How did I get here?

I looked up the hill. It seemed to only get steeper as it disappeared into the clouds. Despite the warm day, there was a low cloud ceiling. I decided the only way to avoid the Skinners would be to make the clouds.

I ran was much as I could. Which wasn't much. I walked when I couldn't, which was often.

I heard voices below me. There was yelling.

I kept going. I would not be caught by no good Skinners. They must be monsters. How can a people force others to remove their skin?

I struggled up and up. The hill, who am I kidding, this was an unnatural mountain. There was no shadow cast upon it. It had perfect grass. Grass you'd only find on the side of a gentle sloping mowed hill. It had just the right grip for walking. Like a golf course.

I continued to climb, but the Skinners were on some sort of flying machine. It seemingly hovered over the ground and allowed them to quickly and easily ascend to be level with me.

I despaired. I could only imagine, in the context of what that first Skeleton had said to me, keep your body, that they would do violence to me. That they would skin me as their name implies.

I heard the earth shudder behind me, "Sir, please stop running. We're here to help."

Now, I'm a god fearing man and I know that some of the most terrifying words ever spoken are "I'm from the government and we're here to help." I wasn't any more calm with the towering skeleton attempting to reassure me.

Another voice cut in, "Sir. We can help you get home. People with bodies like yours cause serious problems here. You need to go home."

I stopped and turned then. There were two other skeletons next to the stone crushing voiced skeleton. I couldn't tell which one was speaking. They were just smiling skulls with no emotions.

I shuddered.

I heard one of them mutter, "God, it repulses me."

The one that offered to help muttered back, "Shut up Steve. We need to gain its trust."

The gravel voiced skeleton sighed. He pulled something out of his pocket. It looked like a gun. I started to scramble away, but felt a sharp pain. It felt like I'd been hit with a paintball.

My vision blurred. I'd been drugged. They drugged me. "You sssssons of bitchesss. You drugged me." I slurred as I stumbled. I felt the world tip. I was on a very steep hill after all.

I began to fall as darkness enveloped me.

I woke up in a bedroom. It looked like mine. I took a deep breath.

There was a knock on the door. A skull faced head popped in, "Oh good, you're awake. Good news! The procedure was a complete success!" The voice sounded like Death, the very first skeleton I'd come across. Death held up a mirror. My skull grinned back at me.

For A Hill

His knees were screaming in pain. His breath was ragged. Sgt. Ali was scared. He could hear the energy beams slam into the dirt just above their foxhole.

They'd been fighting over this stupid patch of ground for weeks now. Upper command never explained why this hill was so damned important for the colonial marines to hold. But here they were.

Ali turned back on the music. The loudspeakers jumped to life. Dozens of energy beams lanced towards the speakers. Ali grinned, his family would be proud. He'd learned this from his own family's history. Apparently during the United States of America's Late hegemonic period, the country invaded his homeland of Iraq and used this sort of music to abuse the locals.

Ali found the music fitting. This one was Metallica's For Whom the Bell Tolls, which describes the hopelessness of fighting for a hill that had no real strategic value. The narrator dies a pointless death.

It wasn't even their most anti-war song, that was One, which does a fantastic job driving the Novines into a frenzy. That one had caused the grunts to turn on some of their leaders.

Heavy metal was doing a lot of work. His men needed the break. His squad was shrinking. He'd lost a trooper yesterday. Another was barely hanging on. Their arm had been blown off during a short counter attack.

Ali radioed to another foxhole, "What's the situation?"

There was a crackle as an energy beam distorted the response, "Repeat, we're under heavy fire. Command is sending reinforcements.

Over."

"Acknowledge. When are we getting relieved. Over."

A dry laugh was his only answer as the transmission was cut.

Ali popped his head up. The enemy was preparing another bombardment. They were setting up their low altitude artillery. It was an interesting weapon. On old Earth, they would have been something similar to Hot Air Balloons. Here, they were anti-grav with some serious shielding. The weapon wasn't intended to survive for long. Just long enough to fire a few shots, then drop on the enemy position. It was a bunker buster itself.

Ali took a few potshots at the device. He switched to a grenade.

He sighed and dropped back into his foxhole. He set his back against the embankment and sobbed. There was nothing his small armament could do against that weapon. He was getting no air support. Ali knew that weapon was to distract from weaponless troop transport. More men to be ground into burger on this fucking hill.

None of it made sense. The marines were making this position look important, so the Novines were treating it like it was important. It was the most worthless hill within 60 kilometers.

Ali keyed the speakers to move to another location. He stopped the worthless autonomous guns from firing. They weren't doing any damage anyway.

He pushed Pvt. Alderman down into the hill. They'd dug out a small room inside the hill to store food and sleep. It helped a lot when things were getting spicy or you were spent.

Ali waited. The anti-grav artillery took off. He could hear it. It blasted the gun positions. They were fine, just like if he'd fired his guns at it. Nothing but wasted energy.

Ali played dead. He used his suit to lower his body temperature. With Alderman in the hill, it looked like there were two corpses in the foxhole.

Ali watched the anti-grav weapon scan his position. It hovered for a while. Collecting whatever data it felt was important. One of the other foxholes must have taken a potshot, because it swung away and suddenly dropped on another location.

He could hear the foxhole's shields repel the buster. He swore.

That damn hole was lucky. His shields went out a week ago.

He must have fallen asleep because he started awake. He heard ships making planet fall. The Novine's energy weapons were firing like crazy.

Ali started up the music, he keyed in One by Metallica. He flashed up the silenced guns and sent them to fire at any position firing at the incoming ships.

He could hear the chaos from the enemy lines. He popped his head up. He smelled burning flesh. He found himself sliding back into the foxhole. He glanced down. His right shoulder was gone. Part of his chest was burned away too.

Ali began to fade to black as he saw a ship land at his foxhole. With his last breath he cursed he couldn't see the skies above Iraq again. He couldn't even see it here, just the belly of another troop transport.

Lonesome

A man is staring into his fire place. He's graying at the temples. His goatee has flecks of gray. The fire crackles invitingly.

The rest of the room is cloaked in dancing shadow. The worn leather chair casts large looming shadows across the back wall. The edges of the chair jut like wings across the back wall.

There's a table next to the chair on which a pair of horn rimmed glasses rests with their legs half folded pressing into a bottle. The bottle has dust covering on its shoulders. There's a hand print in the dust. The label says it's a Laphroig 18. The cork is sitting next to his glasses. there's a smokey aroma emanating from the bottle.

The man's hand is wrapped around a rocks glass. There's condensation dripping onto the armrest.

Ice tinked starling the man. He lifted the glass, swirled the contents, and took a sip. He grimaces as he holds the liquid on his tongue. He'd swallowed by the time he'd replaced the glass on the chair.

The man raises his shaggy eye brows, glittering blue eyes glance at a picture resting on the mantle. It's a happy couple, dancing at their wedding. He's one of the two people in the picture.

He lowers his eyes to the fire, grimacing. He takes another sip.

Rain patters against the windows. The light of the fire feels weak and thin. Rather than illuminating, the light highlights the darkness. The emptiness outside and inside.

A log shifted and sparks leapt up the chimney. The man's eyes followed a stray spark, floating on the plume of smoke, growing dimmer and dimmer, until it winked out.

He clears his throw and puts the glass on the table. He glances down and sees the ring on the arm of his chair. He grunts and wipes it away. Some splashed on the fireplace rocks steam hissed as the water bubbled away.

He grabbed the poker and adjusted the logs. Sent more sparks up the chimney. After he replaced the poker, he leaned forward, nearly out of the chair, and grabs a log. He shifted and tried to find the best place to move the log. He half tossed and half dropped the log.

He fumed when the log rolled from the perfect position. He wrenched the poker and pushed the log back. It's a futile battle, the log can't stay there, but he tried to force it anyway.

He flung the poker back in annoyance and flopped into the back of his chair in one smooth motion.

He held his face as a sob breaks through. After wiping a tear from his cheek, he grabbed the bottle and poured another finger of scotch. His glass was nearly three quarters full of scotch.

He adjust himself in his seat and contemplated the fire. A log popped. He took a long pull from his drink.

A motorcycle roared in the darkness outside. His knuckles whiten on his glass. His eyes darted to the happy couple dancing.

He took a drink, draining much of his glass. He quickly refilled the glass. He slammed the bottle down. He clipped the leg of his glasses. They skittered into the darkness behind the man.

He growled in frustration. He glanced at the picture again.

After taking a sip, he lurches towards the mantel. He grabbed the frame and clumsily worked the back open. He grabbed the picture, crumpled it in his hand. He dropped the frame, shattering the glass. He leaned towards the fire and tossed the picture on.

He sat back. The picture started to uncurl. A picture of a smiling dancing woman stared at him. He lunged for the poker, desperate to fling the picture away from the flames. The picture had already caught. Even out of the direct fire, the fire consumed the picture. Flames slowly moved towards the woman's face. Until it was gone.

The man slid from the chair. The poker bounced on the wooden floor. He held his head as he sobbed.

The fire crackles. The rain patters. Darkness and shadows dance.

Edge of Blackness

He glanced out the window. The inky blackness of space reflected his face back at himself. He saw himself blink. The inky blackness of space wasn't what he was expecting. There should have been a large planet hanging instead of inky blackness.

Sven slid his hand across the edge of the window. Sven snorted to himself, it's not really a window, it's a monitor. As he his hand slid the image changed to a different camera, not that there was much to indicate this other than a few pieces of ship that changed.

Sven frantically swiped through all the different cameras. Nothing but blackness. Sven paused then. His hand centimeters from the edge.

No stars.

There was less than nothing outside of the ship.

Sven pushed a hidden button and a keyboard popped out. The blackness with bits of ship changed to a terminal. Sven navigated to pull up operational controls. He found an outboard drone. He remotely connected a retrieval wire to the drone.

Sources of tension like the tether were always points of rotation for flight in space. The drone would have to account for this as it flew. Not that Sven had any plan other than fly directly away from the ship until the tether stops the drone.

Sven keyed in the program.

He opened multiple camera views and trained them on the drone. On the camera almost directly below the drone, it remained visible. However, on the camera at the bow of the ship, the drone disappeared into the blackness.

As the drone hit the tethered length, it was surrounded in darkness. Sven, saw the darkness move to embrace the drone.

Alarms blared. The drone's camera showed nothing but blackness. The camera cracked, splintering as if it was under massive pressure.

Sven's computer showed the drone had gone offline or at least the signal was lot.

A message appeared on his monitor, "This system is under my protection. Leave and never return."

Stars appeared in a single camera. It was the aft camera.

Sven slammed the "EMERGENCY" button next to the monitor. Klaxon blared throughout the kilometer long ship. Sven was in no position to make that sort of decision.

Sven paced. His face felt flush. He touched his ears, his fingers came away wet. He felt his stomach turn.

He ran to nearest trash receptacle.

"What's this emergency?" Boomed a voice behind him.

It was senior staff. Sweat oozed out of Sven.

"Answer her, young man." called a soothing voice. The crew was still walking towards the bridge, but the airlock had been opened ahead of them.

"Sirs," Sven's voice cracked. He cleared his throat. "I detected an anomaly in space. I only saw blackness. Then I got a message from that blackness."

A voice scoffed, "Blackness in space, imagine that. Probably saw a constellation and got spoked."

"Silence" The captain commanded.

"Yes, Sir." came the tense reply.

Sven punched in a few commands and pulled up the sequence of video the computer automatically recorded. He showed them on the main screen for the full bridge crew to review.

"Did you review the video of when this," the captain hesitated, "Blackness appeared?"

Sven shook his head, "No. I panicked when the blackness sent that message."

She smiled at Sven. Sven felt his shoulders relax then. "You did the right thing, Ensign. Please pull up that information."

"Um, sir. It still has the tether." Sven replied.

"WHAT?"

"I have been attempting to retract the tether since before I got that message. No cable has retracted." Sven coughed, "sir."

She rubbed her chin. "Hmm, Xeno?"

"There have been other systems where there are protectors, but they are usually more aggressive. This is different."

"Security?"

"Destroy it and claim this system as our own."

She sighed, "Operations and Engineering?"

The main screen changed before O&E could respond. Sven replayed the video history. The images showed bits of starts blinking in and out. Then all at once the ship was surrounded. The drone appeared to rocket from the ship. The stars appeared aft out of nothing.

"How long did that envelopment take?" She asked.

Sven swallowed, "According to the computer's analysis, 1 millisecond. The blinking of the stars took place over the span of several hours, which is reflected in the size of the planet."

"Estimated size?"

"At least 15 km3, it's unclear how thick the object is. Based on the drone's penetration, at least several hundred meters." Sven quickly finished with, "Sir."

"O&E, how quickly can we turn?"

"It will take us another hour to turn around and leave. It would be faster if we could accelerate and sling ourselves -"

"Thank you. Helm, chart a course to turn and burn." She stood. After pausing to straighten her uniform, she said, "I'll be in my office. Esign, come with me."

"Sir."

"Please let me know if -" before she could finish the entire vessel had lurched to the side.

A message appeared on the main screen and every other screen on the ship. "YOU HAVE NOT CHANGED COURSE. LEAVE. This planet is under my protection."

"Ensign, can you send a message back?" The Captain asked.

"Sir, I did not try, as I am not permitted to initiate first contact with Xeno-Intelligences. What would you like me to say? Sir."

"Tell the protector that we are in progress of changing course."

Sven keyed his computer and brought up a terminal to send a message to the drone. "Protector we are currently plotting a new course to leave." Sven typed.

The captain nodded tersely. "Helm, get us out of here."

"To whom am I speaking?"

Sven typed, "Captain Olivia Vargas."

"Sir," cried security, "The blackness has closed in around the ship. It is within 250 meters!"

The screen dissolved into a single word, "LIAR."

Sven felt sweat drip in to his eyes, he replied quickly, "Ensign Sven Johanson is literally typing, however, I am taking clear direction from Captain Vargas. I have some latitude to answer and act independently, but I am acting as an extension of her."

Sven felt a hand on his chair. He glanced up and saw Captain Vargas. She nodded. Then she spoke, "Protector, you have us at a disadvantage. It seems you can see everything we do, but we cannot see or know anything about you?"

Sven typed everything verbatim.

The Protector responded, "You know everything *you* need to know about me. These planets are under my protection. And, that you need to leave. I can assume, given our conversation here, that you are able to understand implied threats. Sven, why were you unable to turn around yourself?"

Captain nodded for Sven to answer himself.

"I am not high enough rank. Only Captain Vargas or another senior officer can make that decision in the case she's unable."

"How many senior staff would need to be unable for you to have made this decision."

Sven counted his fingers, then shrugged, "I'm not sure, more than a dozen but probably less than 200."

Captain Vargas suddenly fell to the ground. She was rigid locked into taking a step towards Sven. She'd had one foot in the air when she frozen.

"What would you have done?"

Sven licked his lips. He wiped sweat from his forehead. Security's chair slid out from under him.

"I would have ran, err, left immediately. I could not though."

Sven called to Helm, "When are we getting the fuck out of here?"

Helm called back, "How dare you ask me that? I'm working on it. I've almost got it. Give me five more minutes."

Sven responded through clenched teeth, "You're higher rank than me. If you do that," Sven gestured towards Captain Vargas, "I'll probably end up getting us all killed. Please hurry."

Sven looked about. The air, *felt* as if someone was laughing around him. He squinted at the screen, "Are you laughing at us?" Sven asked.

The feeling increased. Xenobiology frozen.

"Yes, I am laughing. It seems that authority is flexible in your world."

"Authority is only flexible in the moment. You've forced on us that shift in authority. It is very likely that I could be both praised and reprimanded for what's happening here. IF I make things worse, then I'll certainly be reprimanded. If we get out of here, alive, I may be reprimanded for breaking the chain of command by acting above my station."

Sven felt a shift. He was suddenly standing on the drone's tether. He held his breath and shut his eyes. His wrist computer beeped at him.

He opened his eyes and took a tentative breath.

There was more laughter about him. "Smart boy. Noise means air."

Sven narrowed in on the voice. It was a small black ball. No larger than a grape. it was floating no more than a meter in front of him.

"What am I doing here?"

"What were your intentions for this system?" the Grape asked.

Sven shrugged, "Me personally? This is my job. My job is to make sure that ship, down that tether, gets to where its supposed to. That ship's intention, or the intention imbued in our mission, is to deliver colonists to one of the inner planets and get them set up here. Then we would leave and continue towards another system to scout it out."

"Why?"

"Why what?"

"Why would you leave colonists?"

"After almost destroying our planet, we decided not to leave all our eggs in one basket. Better to have people all over space, than just on one planet. Plus, humans like to explore and live in hostile environments."

"This system is under my protection. Would you still leave colonists?"

"No. We never leave colonists where there's a clear Class 3 or greater species. You are at least a class 5 species."

Air returned to a sense of laughter. "Such a foolish scale. You seek dominion over class 2 and lower? Do you seek to prevent more class 3 from emerging?"

The grape shot into Sven. It moved faster than his eye could see. One moment it was there, the next it was gone.

Sven gasped and shifted.

The ship lurched. The tether was suddenly retracting.

Captain Vargas groaned. Security dizzily sat up, blood was streaming from his forehead.

Helm was busy, he suddenly leaned back sighing with relief. "Sorry Captain, I had to use some emergency maneuvers and spike the Gs well above the safety range for our passengers. I can't be sure they all will have survived." Helm cried.

Sven felt himself being thrust to the side. His body spoke then, "Captain Vargas. You should commend this vessel. Sven did very well for you and your species."

"What have you done with Ensign Sven?" Captain Vargas growled.

"He's still here. I'm a Protector. Never come back here. Do not let any other ship visit this system. If you do, I will expand my area of protection far beyond this system. I understand you intend to live with species on planets you colonize. If I learn that is not the truth of things, I will expand my sphere of protection. Until then, I have my passion project here."

Captain Vargas's jaw worked as she tried to formulate a reply.

"The protector's gone." Sven said. He held his head. "Such a beautiful project." Sven whimpered. He looked back up at Captain Vargas, "Please, tell the Earth Force Federation. Make them listen. We do not want to become the next passion project."

A Dark God

Douglas decided it was time for him to step out of the darkness. to take his rightful place in the world again.

He smiled as he looked at the little people studying his home. They had these little brushes, large wide brimmed hats, and sacks with pieces of chalk and string. The leader of these people looked to be examining his alter. He was making some notes in a little book.

"Have you found anything interesting?" Douglas asked him, while peering over the man's shoulder at his book.

"Holy shit, where did you come from?" the man yelped.

"I came from the shadows." Douglas gestured towards a darkened alcove under the main icon of skulls and bones.

The man had a hand against his chest he was breathing rapidly. He took a breath and swallowed, "Yes, right, but before the shadows. Did you sneak up the stairs?"

Douglas laughed. It was a dry laugh, like papers shuffling. "No, nothing like that. You see this is my temple. These people worshipped me."

The man scoffed, "You, right."

Douglas shrugged, "What did you have to say about Olivia? My she was a pretty one." He gave a look at the man, "I really argued with Thorgen not to sacrifice her." Douglas sighed and shook his head, "There was no reasoning with Thorgen, he was convinced that building this." Douglas gestured around, "Would stop the end of their world." Douglas sadly shook his head.

The man was staring at him. The man blinked a few times,

"Thorgen, I'd only just translated this disc." He held up a bronze disc looped around a leather thong.

"Well, Jimmy. I'm sorry, do you mind if I call you Jimmy?" Douglas asked, somewhat blandly.

"Oh, you wanted a reply, no well, that is. How did you know my name?" the man named Jimmy asked.

"I told you, this is my temple. I'm so sorry. My name is Douglas." Douglas held out his hand for Jimmy to shake.

Without thinking Jimmy took his hand, absently shook it.

Douglas smiled, "I'm the god of death. I'm pleased that you find what my friends left behind. I was getting lonely. Many of them have been crying, about some betrayal, for what feels like no end." He waved his hand dismissively.

A young person came up to Jimmy, they said, "Jimmy, who's this?"

Jimmy cleared his throat, "Dom, this is Douglas. He lives here."

"Him? Where, there's no bed. Why would an accountant be living out here." They looked confused.

Douglas reached out his hand, "Pleasure to meet you Dom!"

Dom glanced down at it, "Sorry, I don't shake hands. The world I grew up on had a chronic plague. I'm sure you understand." Dom shrugged.

Douglas broke into a huge, "A plague world?" he said dreamily. "So, many lives to count and categorize."

"You're a creepy ass accountant." Dom muttered.

"Dom, let me ask you a question. Don't you think an accountant is a fantastic aspect of Death? Counting and reviewing every aspect of life. Every life. Someone has to determine if a world is worth living, right?" Douglas queried.

Dom stopped in their tracks, "What do you mean?"

Douglas gestured towards the disc in Jimmy's hand, "Now, there you have Thorgen deciding the ONLY way to save the world is to sacrifice more and more people to me. To build an alter and temple from the corpses of the sacrifices. How does one judge those choices" Douglas cried.

Dom stared at him. Jimmy coughed, "Is that a serious question?"

Douglas nodded vigorously.

Dom's eyes got huge. They tried to blink. Bring themselves back to reality.

Jimmy sighed, "Well, that's a tough question. Could you manifest like this to them?"

Douglas nodded, "Yes, but they never listened to me. I would tell them to stop killing people, but they REFUSED to believe their god was actually named Douglas. Well, their translated version of Douglas, of course. They had some ridiculous name for me, like Doomhammer the Bone Forge."

Dom nodded, "You can blame the old and the conservatives. Reformers and victims were not at fault. You needed to judge each person by their own actions."

Douglas rubbed his chin. He gestured towards Olivia's bones, "Ok, sure. Olivia there was both a victim and a perpetrator. She sacrificed her unborn child to me! What? Who would do that?"

Behind Dom a voice called out, "What did you do to them?!"

Douglas turned around. "What do you mean?" He took a step forward and tripped over Jimmy. "Oh, I get it."

He waved his hands. Dom and Jimmy gasped for breath. He muttered, "Sorry" as he stepped back into the shadows, lost in thought.

***

Dom was skittish as they ascended back up to the alter. It'd been over a week since their literal brush with death. They peered into every shadow and carried multiple lanterns and torches to make sure Douglas couldn't appear to surprise them.

The base doctor had checked them out and there was nothing wrong. Well, there was a strange scar and a freshly healed fracture but that was it. The scar was shaped like a hammer and chisel. The fracture looked a bit like a forge, but probably was just a tablet of stone.

Dom was going back up to see if they could detect any presence of Douglas. Not that they wanted to experience that again, but they were certainly marked by the experience. The expedition had found scriptures referring to those marked. They had been given the Hammer of Doom. In almost all cases those individuals were ritually sacrificed.

Dom surmised all of them had been visited by Douglas and had "survived" the experience. The people of this world, decided they should die for that. Dom was setting up their work station. They had just set up a camera and was looking through the viewfinder.

"Ok, so you know. I talked with Olivia. It appears she did not actually sacrifice her unborn child to me. I, uh, revived it outside of her body." Douglas's voice came from the wall.

Dom glanced up. He was right there. They could see him, but the camera couldn't. "Fuck" Dom muttered. Then they registered what Douglas said, "Holy shit that's fucked up, what's wrong with you?!" they strung the words together into a single long word.

Douglas shrugged, "I've never had a child before. Didn't understand the mechanics then and don't really now." He eyed them up and down, "can you have one? maybe i can...."

"None of your business and whatever you are thinking no. My body. Mine. You violated my bodily autonomy once by doing this." They pulled up their sleeve to reveal the Hammer of Doom.

"Huh," Douglas said, "Wonder if that's where they get my name from."

"How fucking oblivious are you?" Dom cried.

"Hold on, you have to understand, there were a lot of people dying. I was trying to understand what was happening. I asked a lot of people. Next thing I know, they stop worshiping the sun and build this monstrosity to me."

"What was killing them?" Dom asked.

"Oh, they were killing themselves. They fucked up this planet so bad it was rejecting them like you might reject a donor organ." Douglas shrugged, "Wasn't anything I could do. I usually had a pretty stately job. Sure it was getting busier in a linear fashion even with the exponential population growth, but I could plan for that. Then BOOM, tipping point, crash."

Douglas sighed, "Now I just track animals. Don't get me wrong, those are interesting to track, but their lives are so boring compared to the likes of Bronty here. What a life!"

Douglas had picked up a skull and was staring into the eyes.

Dom took a few steps back, "I'm sure it's much less interesting here now. What do you plan on doing?"

Douglas gave them a quizzical look, "Doing? Whatever do you mean? This planet is alive and vibrant and will eventually have interesting life again. I got a taste of your life and WOO Wee. SPACE TRAVEL! Your people's chronic plagues. Your home world is on the brink!"

Dom stared at him, "Are you going to stay here or are you going to try to leave?"

Douglas looked at the stars wistfully, "I'd love to leave, but I can't. The suffering I'd leave in my wake would be criminal. Every god in the universe would hunt me down. Can you image a world where Death abandoned their post? The poor animals would be alive as their bodies failed them. Leaving them in never ending pain."

Douglas looked at Dom, "No, I will not do that. Death is awful for you living. I have learned that much. I do what I can to ease their anger, but there's not much I can do."

Dom swallowed hard, "What would you do if my people came here en mass?"

"Kill you all." Douglas laughed, "eventually." He shrugged and glanced about. "I'll have to chat with death fragment you brought with you. I'm sure we'll come to some sort of agreement."

Dom started as he disappeared. They glanced at their other arm, a matching scar. They staggered to the ground with a wracking sob.

Umhat

Umhat felt the shockwave, the second, and then the earth trembled. He turned to his crew. They were loaded in the bike's cargo hold, they were ready. Umhat nodded and began to pedal.

He raced. Getting there first was critical for the success of the colony. Getting there first, but making sure there was enough for the others was critical.

The bike's windings boosted his power, allowing him to ride faster. His custom designed suspension allowed them to glide over the shattered remains of the great Stone Trees. The wake of the Great Ones was always treacherous.

Umhat could smell their prize before he could see it. He heard whoops behind him. Umhat glanced over his shoulder and smiled at the bugs behind them.

Umhat whooped and upped his tempo. The more time he had before the bugs got there, the better off both groups would be. The bugs would only share if people got their first, but would not tolerate if people took everything.

Rather than breaking, Umhat found a relatively clear section near their prize, and swung the bike around, using the wheels to break the momentum. As soon as the bike had slowed, the crew leapt out. Fulan was still fumbling with her mask. She wasn't holding on and got flung into the massive pile of Great One shit.

Umhat hopped from his seat and pulled up his mask in one fluid motion. He sprinted to her. He pulled her out as quickly as he could. She wasn't conscience. Umhat sprinted away from the fecal prize and went to work.

He pulled any matter from her nose and throat. He poured water over her along with a mixture of alcohol and bicarbonate that helped dissolve the matter. She sputtered and took a ragged breath.

Umhat patted her shoulder, "Oh thank the Stonewood. I thought you were gone."

Fulan smiled weakly, "Thank you." She tried to stand, but wobbled and plopped on her backside. She glanced at Umhat ruefully, "I'm not going to be much good today."

Umhat pulled her up, "Nonsense. You get to help me with the bugs."

Fulan shuddered, "Can't I go play in the shit?"

Umhat smiled, "You know the rules. You can't go near that for at least a month." He gestured towards his mask, "Get your mask on. Can't have you pass out again. Bugs might get you." He grinned evilly. Fulan blanched, she quickly pulled up her mask.

Umhat returned to the crew. They were working hard. They'd set up a perimeter around the section they wanted to gather. The bug portion was necessarily larger. Fortunately, this was a massive find. There would be more than enough for everyone.

Umhat heard another crew arrive behind him as he was walking past while Fulan gave her crew an apologetic wave. Umhat reached the demarcation point just as the largest bug stood on its hind legs. It was easily twice the height of Umhat.

Umhat bowed, "My Lord Jundar." Umhat had no need to saw the words, it was mostly for Fulan.

The bug, Jundar, was as difficult as ever to read. The exo-skeleton doesn't allow freedom of expression like a face does, though, the bugs only thought faces were good for eating.

Jundar's antenna did twitch in greeting. One pointed towards Fulan. Both humans felt the impression of intent, "Who is this interloper. Oh, she nearly overindulged." ~humor~ "You show great restraint." ~surprise~ "Instead of taking equal portions you leave even more for us." ~magnanimous~ "We will continue to honor our treaty." ~suspicion~ "Though we expect betrayal at any moment."

Umhat smiled, though Jundar couldn't understand it. "Thank you for your continued enforcement of the treaty. We have made great effort to make up for past failings. We will continue to strive to avoid future hostilities."

Jundar lowered both antennas "You humans have come far, but we are not a trusting species." ~caution~ "The Great Ones are uneasy. Be wary. Good hunting".

Jundar turned and the other bugs went to work. They adhered exactly to the perimeter. The humans worked their portion more slowly. Umhat took one cargo bin back, the ride was long and challenging. Even though the village tried to keep up with the Great Ones, it was often impossible. They simply walked too fast.

Umhat had just returned from a trip to the village when another rider hailed him.

"Umhat, the elders are summoning you." The young woman said.

Umhat wiped his brow, "Seriously, why didn't they just ask me to stay in the village?"

She shrugged, "Must have just missed you. Leave your bike with Fulan and me. You'll take mine. You need to ride to Village Oleary."

Umhat paused and gave her a look, "Why Oleary? I've been doing runs to Village Gomez. Is that why we missed each other?"

She shook her head, "Oleary is closest to the incident. Something's going on with the Great Ones. Good luck sir and great work here." She gave him a winning smile and blinked rapidly.

Umhat sighed, "Yea, thanks. What's your name?"

She looked startled. He continued, "So I can explain who sent me."

She looked crestfallen, "My name is Tuin."

He smile, "Thanks Tuin. Good luck with the next load of shit."

He adjusted the seat of her bike and took off. He checked the water and food in his pack as he was riding. "Fuck." He breathed. Just barely enough to make it there.

Without his enhancements, the ride was rough going. Oleary was on the other side of the Great Ones - literally. Gomez was southernly while Oleary was Northernly of the Great Track. The Jundese river was between the two villages. Jundar's people lived along the river. As far as Umhat knew, Jundar had been alive since humans settled the planet. Jundar claimed to be ageless.

It was nearing dusk when Umhat reached the Jundese river. Umhat fell off his bike, he had bonked. He gasped for air and held his head. After a few minutes of rest, he felt a little less bottomed out so he reached for a bottle of water. He fell over.

Admitting defeat, he crawled the rest of the way to get the water. He drank greedily. He sputtered, then coughed. Hydrated, Umhat sat. He was lighted headed, still, so he rocked as he stared at the river. There was no way he could cross this tonight. Not feeling like this and not with the low light.

Umhat glanced about. There wasn't much cover here. The Great Ones had already been through. They were moving quicker than normal. Umhat pulled some dried potatoes from his bag. He chewed on those while staring at the river.

As he chewed the river sound grew louder and louder. It sounded like thrumming wings. Umhat shook himself from his exhaustion and looked up.

One of the bugs. Jundar's people. It was rare to see one of the fliers. which was good for the humans. Fliers could get the Great One's leavings before any human could hope to.

Umhat dragged himself to his feet as the flier landed. He bowed. He needed to steady himself as he stood. His vision narrowed from the effort.

It was then Umhat heard Jundar's voice, "You look tired and weaker than normal" ~concern~ "Did your effort to get here exhaust you?"

Umhat nodded, "Yes, it did, sir." Umhat drew a hand down his face, maybe it was the exhaustion or maybe it was familiarity, but he asked the boldest question of his life, "Why do you sound like Jundar? You don't look anything like the Jundar I met this morning."

"You humans are still so very ignorant of this world. We," the bug made a very human gesture and raised an arm up and down its body, "are a hive mind. Jundar is a faction of the mind that interacts with you, specifically." "Did you really think that was the same body every time?"

Umhat thought back to the last few times they'd met, "You know, there were some pretty significant differences, like missing legs, that I'd just ignored. Sorry."

~pleasure~ "No offense given. I'm glad you saw the Jundar of each body rather than the body each time." ~curiosity~ "Since you humans are not a hive mind, why did they bring you here?"

Umhat absently took a bite of his potato. "I was summoned to Oleary." Umhat gestured towards the village. "I'm one of our fastest riders and I've been around the Great Ones a good deal. They wanted me to investigate an incident."

"Excellent. I am please to deal with you."

"Deal with me?" confusion crossed Umhat's face.

"Oh, yes. We requested a human to view the incident with us. I recommended you."

Umhat felt the air move about them. Then the thrum of more wings. He looked up. More fliers.

~assertive~ "We are trusting you. You must trust us. We will take you to Oleary, as you call the tree, we call Vital Blackness."

Umhat swallowed, "You're going to carry me there?"

"Yes."

Umhat took a deep breath and looked at the black line of the river next to him. "Ok." he breathed.

As soon as he consented, Jundar rushed forward and grabbed him. It launched into the air and flew quickly. Much quicker than Umhat had never ridden his bike. He could barely catch his breath.

As Umhat adjusted, he was able to take in the flight. It was riveting to be moving like this. Now he understood the gliders. They moved from village to village lifted on the thermals. They had a mission to try to regain communication with the ship.

Umhat saw that one of the bugs had taken his bike for him. At first he was a bit concerned, but noted the care the bug handled it with. Umhat smiled.

"We are glad you are pleased with our handling of you and your equipment." Jundar impressed the thoughts upon Umhat.

"Thank you for treating it with respect. Those bikes are difficult to make with the tools we have."

~comforting~ "Please relax. You are safe."

Umhat did his best to relax. The grip Jundar held him in was both secure, but not easy to rest into.

~informational~ "We are arriving. You fell into a sleeping state."

Umhat glanced about confused. After blinking a few times, he saw the village, Oleary or Vital Blackness as Jundar called it. "Thank you for waking me."

People were scurrying about as they approached. They were yelling and pointing. A few were grabbing weapons.

"Can you lift me up so I can easily use my arms?"

"Yes." ~command~ "Calm the humans."

Umhat was shifted higher with his arms visibly untouched by the bug. He waved his arms, indicting to put the weapons down.

"This would be much easier if you could talk without vocalizing."

Jundar set down well out of range of the humans. Another bug returned Umhat's bike. He quickly mounted the bike and sprinted towards the village.

"Stand down," He cried. "They were helping!"

The people milled about. Eventually one, a young woman, stepped forward, "Who is that?"

Umhat slowed as he approached, "This is Umhat Gomez. I was summoned by this village. Jundar decided to help me get here."

The woman raised her eye brows and mouthed "Jundar helped?" She shook her head, "Come this way and bring one of the bugs. The rest will come no closer than the glider landing pad. Is that clear?"

Umhat nodded. He turned his bike and sent an impression to Jundar, "They welcome one body and request the remainder come no closer than where most humans stand."

~irritation~ "Your people are most irrational. I will come."

The bug that had carried Umhat leapt next to Umhat in a blink of the eye. The people on the glider pad cried out, but made no threatening movements.

Umhat pedaled his way through the crowd. Jundar easily kept pace. The young woman had to jog to keep up. She directed Umhat to the village long house.

The long house was one of the few buildings constructed out of Stonewood trees. They had decided to cut the pieces into similar sized blocks. Which resulted in a sort of log cabin and large block aesthetic, unique to long houses in most villages.

Umhat was directed in and Jundar followed. There was another bug in the long house along with a number of elders from more than a few villages. Including a few interior villages.

One of the elders chuckled, "You were right. How did you know?"

"Ask Umhat after this is dealt with" replied the bug in the long house.

Elder Gomez spoke then, "Thank you for coming Umhat. I see another emissary of the Jundanese found you."

Umhat smiled, "Yes. Now what's this about?"

"We need you to investigate very strange behavior of the Great Ones. They have gone to the coast. They've never done this before. You and this bug will go in the morning."

Umhat groaned. "I don't have any of my equipment."

"You will have everything you need. We will get whatever your people cannot provide." Jundar replied.

Umhat shrugged. "Ok. Fine." He quickly imprinted exactly what equipment he needed from Gomez.

He glanced at the elders, "Show me where the Great Ones have gone."

The next morning, before sunrise, Umhat woke. He quickly dressed and walked to the village community mess. There was a hearty breakfast of eggs, potatoes, hot cakes, and more. But most importantly, coffee.

As he exited, Jundar joined him. "Your equipment is on the glider pad. Let us go."

Umhat bowed, "I'm sorry for causing a delay. Gotta eat, though."

Umhat inspected his equipment. It was all there. His favorite hatchet, bow, and machete. His bike was in perfect condition. This wasn't the bike he'd gotten yesterday or his cargo bike, this was his proper adventure bike. Large wheels, organic gearing that could adjust to climb anything. Bags for holding weeks worth of food and water.

He turned to Jundar, "Thank you, this is" Umhat hesitated, "perfect." He grinned from ear to ear.

~dismissal~ "of course. this is what you requested." ~annoyance~ "Let us go now. You may not have much need of this."

The pair left Oleary in the more traditional manner. Umhat rode down the spiraling ramp, while Jundar flew down and met him at the bottom.

They began their trek across the wilderness. The sun was yet to rise and with the canopy above, they would be traveling in a half lit twilight until they found the Greath Ones' path.

About an hour in, Jundar stopped. "I believe we are far enough away. Please ride right there." Jundar gestured to a specific spot.

Umhat shrugged and rode there and dismounted. The ground immediately shifted under him. He felt himself lift up.

He was on a giant bug. It was a long many legged bug. It spoke to him, "You will ride me. This will be faster than you riding or the hive carrying you. Lie down."

Umhat lowered his bike to the ground and laid down next to it. He held his machete tight. His knuckles white.

"I know this is a change of plans. We need to get there quickly and this is the only way. I am trusting you. Your people know nothing about the greater variety of me."

"Are you every insect on this planet?" Umhat whispered, terrified. "Are you the bugs we eat too?"

~informational~ "There are more than one hive minds on Mother." ~dismissive~ "We will not speak of those bugs now. That is another discussion. One we don't have time for."

The monstrous bug shifted, its carapace closed around Umhat. He heard a seal. Despite the shell, the air was clean and the space was large enough to move about.

Umhat felt drowsy.

~gentle command~ "Sleep now."

Umhat stirred. He opened his eyes to see the sun. That large white orb in the sky. It was too low. He started. He sat up and stared about. The ocean. He was already at the coast. He was high. Very high.

~greeting~ "Good you're awake. You are at the top of one of the Sky Trees." Jundar was the flier again.

Umhat looked down. The tree seemed to be floating. Part of the tree was above the clouds.

Umhat heard a great crash. He glanced about, but couldn't see what the source of the noise was. Jundar didn't provide any information. Jundar seemed to be looking off towards a distant rock outcropping.

Umhat squinted. There were Great Ones there. They were doing something.

The tree swayed.

Umhat reached into his bike bag. He pulled out a telescope. He focused on the Great Ones. They were tearing into the earth. There were much smaller beings running around the Great Ones. If the Great Ones were humans they might be considered children, but these were just smaller, not immature looking.

A spout of lava shot out of the rock outcropping. A great one slammed into the back of the outcropping. Seconds later Umhat heard the crash, moments after, he felt it.

Umhat's voice shook, "What are they doing?"

~terrified~ "Making a weapon." ~uncomfortable~ "Correction, making weapons." The bug pointed along the coast.

Umhat scanned the coastline, there were a number of rocky outcroppings with similar activities. He saw a number of Great Ones swimming out to sea. "Where are they going?"

~alarm~ "They are trying to find the source. The source of the waves." ~terror~ "The waves might wake up their mother." ~anger~ "Are more of your people landing?"

"I don't know. We can't communicate with them." Umhat shook his head, "The Great Ones made sure of that." He finished bitterly.

~considering~"The last time the Great Ones acted like this, your ancestors landed." ~thoughtful~ "That was some 200 circumnavigations ago." ~query~ "Can your people communicate with the ship?"

Umhat shrugged, "I, uh, I'm not sure. The gliders try, but I don't know if they can. 200 circumnavigations, huh, yea, we'd call that 200 years ago, the Great Ones destroyed all our technology, well lectric, including most our coms."

~annoyance~ "Yes, wave creators were destroyed." ~awe~ "The Great Ones were generous, generous enough not to destroy you. They were very afraid. They carry a heavy burden." ~irritated~ "We are blind here."

"What burden?"

~exhaustion "Preventing the awakening of their Mother and Father. They strive to prevent the destruction of my mother. The planet." ~directive~ "We must help them. Humans are obligated to help. Great Ones kept you alive to help. Stop this."

Umhat nodded.

The great crashing stopped. Umhat focused his Telescope on the rocky outcropping. The Great Ones were sitting. Their shoulders slumped. Some had their heads down.

~hopeful~ "The crisis may have been adverted."

The pair continued to observe the Great Ones. Eventually night fell. The sun was big and bright the full day. A novel experience for Umhat. One that his skin did not appreciate. Despite precautions, his face felt hot and stretched.

He leaned back staring into the sky. Counting stars. One of his favorite hobbies. He looked for the blinking light of the ship. This time of the year it would be nearly over head. It was the bicentennial of the first landing, typically the ship was overhead, as Gomez was the first landing location.

Umhat blinked. There was a second light next to the first. This light was much larger than the first. Did another ship arrive? Are more colonists going to land? Is this a misinformed war party?

"Jundar, can you talk with the Great Ones?" Umhat asked.

~cautioned concern~ "Why?"

"I think we're in trouble." Umhat pointed at the sky.

"What is that? A new star?"

"No." He said quietly, "More humans."

Umhat started at the crash of the earth. The skytree swayed. He sat up, he could see fire pouring into the ocean.

Quite the Trip

Elane pushed her daughter into school. Allyson was a freshman in high school, she'd been paralyzed by her drunkard father. Makalya walked next to Elane, she wasn't too happy about walking into school, her first day of high school, with her mother. Elane was tired. It had been a struggle, but she needed to know that Allyson would be taken care of. This was an older building and some of the older buildings just weren't ADA compliant yet.

Elane gave each of her daughters quick glances. She couldn't help but beam with pride. They had both been chosen to attend the prestigious art school. Their bags were filled with art supplies.

Elane jumped in surprise, a young man with shaved head ran by. He'd slapped her ass.

"Did he just slap your butt, mom?" Macalya asked, mortified.

"Yes, he did." Elane replied.

"Steven!" a voice called from behind him. The butt slapper turned heaving a huge sigh, knowing he'd been caught. "You will apologize immediately to this woman and her daughters or I will see you in my office."

Elane turned to see the school principle walking behind them. She glanced at Macalya, who was busy trying to hide her face.

The teenage boy walked back to the trio who were being joined by Principle Walker. He mumbled something that Elane couldn't catch.

"Steven, you need to speak up." Principle Walker tersely stated.

"I'm sorry ma'am. I will not slap you or any other person's butt in the future. If I do, I will be punished by cleaning all the whiteboards and writing a report on intersectionality." Steven said louder this time.

Elane, "I accept your apology." Steven turned and ran off before she'd even finished her sentence.

Elane looked at Principle Walker, "What was with his punishment, how would he know that?"

Principle Walker sighed, "He got that last year. He seems not to have learned that "boys will be boys" is not tolerated here." Principle Walker moved towards Allyson, she knelt to get to Allyson's level, "You must be Allyson. I know we have an older building, but I will happily walk you through all the ADA features the school has."

Principle Walker turned to Macalya, "It's a pleasure to meet you Macalya. If you'd like you can run ahead to your home room while we get your sister situated. I know you're in very different classes."

Macalya glanced at her mother. Elane nodded. That was all the encouragement Macalya needed. She took off at a brisk walk.

After a 20 minute meeting with Principle Walker Elane headed out of the school. It'd started raining. She didn't have an umbrella. It was pouring rain. Elane was drenched by the time she reached her car. Her drive from the school to the house was about 20 minutes. She started to feel strange by the time she got home. Something felt really off.

As she got out of her car, she noticed something sticking to her seat. She pulled it off the seat, it looked like some sort of sheet. She noticed that there were dosing labels.

She rushed to her computer and did some quick Google Sleuthing. It looked like a sheet of LCD. That kid, Steven, had put a small sheet of LCD on her back. Something like 5 doses.

"Fuck." Elane breathed. "What the fuck am I going to do."

She was really starting to feel out of sorts. She decided she was going to sleep it off. So, she went to her bedroom, got in some PJs and turned on the TV. She only caught a quick glance at whatever was playing before she shut her eyes. She realized a moment later, it was an Oompa Loompa.

Elane laid on the bed. The sheets were vibrating beneath her, trying to carry her somewhere. She opened her eyes and found herself in a poorly lit space. She heard lights flick on, boom, boom, boom. Under each light was an Oompa Loompa.

Elane screamed, "Why the fuck are you in my house?"

The Oompa Loompa closest to her started to dance, wagging its finger at her. "What will you get if you stay with your man?"

The back one replied, "Another black eye from the back of his hand?"

The middle one joined in, "What will you get if you stay on the boat?"

Elance looked down, she was on a boat, or more accurately, her bed was floating on a river. The sheets spilling over the foot of the bed seemed to bee pulling her upstream.

The first Oompa Loompa interrupted her inspection. "You'll get this ticket." He held his hand up, it looked to be a lottery ticket.

The boat suddenly swept Elane down stream. She tried to pull on the sheets and comforter, but she couldn't wrest them out of the water.

The left wall suddenly lit. Massive shadows were cast on the wall. It looked like there were four people walking. She glanced down to find the source of the shadows. They were four little people made out of grass, marching in place on the edge of her bed. The light was coming from her side. She rubbed at her stomach and the light shone through her fingers.

She swatted at the grass people, but they jumped to avoid her hand. It wasn't as much of a jump as that they were suddenly above where her hand was and then back on the bed. As if they just weren't where she was.

She noted that as she turned to swing, the light didn't follow her body. It was shining through her. Through the bed onto the grasspeople.

One of the grass people suddenly was in a wheel chair.

Elane stopped struggling and stared at the figures. She got closer to see the details. She could see her own long legs. Despite being shorter than her husband, her legs were longer than his. Macalya took after Elane with very long legs. She'd be a good runner if she decided to join track.

Allyson's legs were already shriveling in the wheel chair. They were looking older, no longer just freshman in high school. They looked a few years older.

Elane felt the boat rock. She looked up and saw a Y in the river ahead of her. The Left path was dark. There was a light on the right side.

Elane tried to pull the bed towards the right side, but instead of veering right, she felt herself split in two. Half of her mind went in each direction. She was seeing the bed from above while going in both directions.

Elane shook her head. She held her head and shut her eyes. She tried to pull herself together, but the images were still split. Still moving. There wasn't much she could do. So, she watched both at once. On the left, her husband got fatter. Elane was suddenly in a cast. Then it was black.

On the right, Elane suddenly pushed away the Husband. She pushed Allyson forward. Her daughters had graduation caps. Then university T-Shirts. Then more graduation caps. Allyson was walking.

Both girls were suddenly walking with other people, Allyson with a feminine form while Macalya walked with a more masculine form. Both soon held children.

Elane still only saw black to the left. It was cold on the left. Smelled of earth. A worm crawled across Elane's vision as the two girls were celebrating something on the right side.

Elane vomited. The grass people scattered. She was back in her bed. Vomit covered her PJs.

She ran to the toilet. She vomited again and again.

She showered. She was in a daze. She could feel the water walking down her skin. She saw little beds flowing down the drain with the water.

The warm water hugged her.

She dried herself off and grabbed her soiled PJs from the floor. She started to ball them up, but felt something solid in the pocket. It looked like the ticket the Oompa Loompa had showed her.

It was a lottery ticket, one of those scratch mega millions ticket. It'd been scratched. It was a winner.

Just Out of Sight

Kevin did a double take. He'd seen something out of the corner of his eye, again. It was happening more and more often. Kevin shook his head. There was nothing to be done about it.

Kevin went on about his day. It was routine, clean the toilet, collect the feminine hygiene products, empty the trash. It was another late night shift at King's Family Restaurant. He glanced at the mirror. Something had been there, in the mirror. Now it was just his face. He could see the crows feet at his eyes. There was gray streaking through his beard and black hair.

How could he still be doing this shit work at 39? Kevin sighed and grabbed the stuffed garbage bag. It was full, stretching the flimsy plastic to its limits. It had been a busy day at the outlet mall. That fucking mall was a plague.

As he left the bathroom, he collected the "Closed For Cleaning sign" and ignored the scowl from the old white woman that smelled of too much perfume. She was obviously trying to cover up some other body odor.

Kevin repressed a shudder as she screeched, "It's about time." He heard her mutter under her breath, "Black people are so lazy."

Kevin clenched the bag tighter, his knuckles turned white.

He walked past the cash register where his manager was chatting with the hostess, Kevin noticed her name tag was red - she was a minor. Kevin sighed. She'd be leaving soon, it was almost ten. She lit up when she saw Kevin. Not because she liked Kevin, but because he always saved her from their creepy manager.

"Hey, Jim." Kevin said loudly.

Jim let out a heavy breath. It spoke volumes. "What do you want, Kevin?" Jim sounded annoyed.

"Little white lady in the bathroom was racist. You should make her leave." Kevin said bluntly.

"Look, Kevin. We've been over this. If we had every racist white person from Western Pennsylvania leave, we'd have no business." Jim rolled his eyes at the hostess.

Sarah, made a disgusted noise. "Jim, you're gross. Oh, look it's 10, time for me to clock out." Sarah mouthed, "Thank you." To Kevin.

Kevin nodded and picked up his bag of trash. As he turned away from Jim and Sarah, he saw something flicker out of the corner of his eye.

He glanced back, there was a darkness enveloping Jim. Reaching out towards Sarah. Tendrils were caressing her.

"I can walk you to your car." Jim said. There was a light sheen on his forehead.

"I'm already heading out to drop this off, Jim. I can make sure she gets to her car safely." Kevin interjected.

Jim turned towards Kevin. The whites of his eyes were black and the pupils were white. "No need Kevin. You need to get bags from the Kitchen, she needs to go before then." Jim turned to Sarah, "Come on. Let's get you home."

Sarah gave Kevin a pleading look. Kevin tried to give her a reassuring look, but ended up shrugging more than reassuring.

Jim gestured towards the front entrance. Sarah deftly moved to avoid his touch. She was way too young to have perfected that subtle dance. Kevin moved towards the back of the restaurant. He noticed other employees were looking towards Jim and Sarah. A few of the women had concerned looks on their faces.

Marrissa grabbed Kevin's arm as he passed, "Do something." She hissed at him. Kevin returned a tight nod.

"Follow me out the back. You know how this could go for me." Kevin muttered.

He rushed out the back door with the trash. He heard a scream. He sprinted towards the source of it.

Jim was forcing himself on Sarah. Right there in the middle of the god damned parking lot. There was a bus full of Asian tourists pulling into the parking lot from the Mall. Kevin saw a few camera flashes.

Kevin grabbed Jim and threw him to the ground. Sarah sobbed. Kevin heard her slide down the car.

Jim threw himself at Kevin. He seemed to grow in size. Wings of darkness unfurled behind Jim. Fire blazed from Jim's eyes as he threw a punch.

Kevin tried to dodge, but his knees weren't in the based shape. Old soccer injuries. Jim's punch was a glancing blow, but still managed to cut Kevin.

Kevin countered with a body blow. Using Jim's momentum against him. Kevin cried out in pain, something gave in his hand. He'd punched walls that were softer than Jim's abs.

Jim staggered back. He drew himself up. He seemed to tower over Kevin, the restaurant, and the bus.

Behind him, Kevin heard Marrissa whispering to Sarah. Encouraging the girl to get out of the way.

Marrissa stood next to Kevin, "What the fuck is that?"

Kevin sighed in relief, "You can see that too? Thank god. He looks like a balrog, that thing Gandalf fought in Lord of the Rings."

Kevin could feel the look Marrissa was giving him, "That was a book, this is -" She cut off as Jimrog launched at them.

He sprinted at them, darkness trailed behind him, like a smoky sail.

Kevin knew there wasn't much he could do. Jim was easily 10 feet tall now. What Kevin still had, though, was a trash bag. He dodged Jim enough to retrieve it.

Poor Sarah's car was destroyed. Marrissa was able to avoid Jim, because Jim was focused on Kevin.

Kevin grabbed the bag and threw it into Jim's face. The bag tore. The contents, while mostly paper towels and tampons, combusted.

Jim cried in fury. It was enough for the three of them to get back past Jim and back inside.

Kevin cried to the patron's, "Get out the back! We're being attacked! GO."

People stared at him in disbelief. The bitter old white lady began to laugh at him.

"Marrissa, grab some knives and whatever you can find from the kitchen. Maybe get the glove for the mandolin." Kevin ordered. "Sarah, get these people out of here. They'll listen to you."

Both Marrissa and Sarah nodded.

Kevin grabbed the mop from his cart. It wasn't going to do much, but it was better than punching that monster again.

Jimrog barged through the front door, shattering the glass, as Kevin grabbed the mop. The patrons screamed behind him. Kevin slammed the soaking mop into the top of Jimrog's head. The fire there went out. Jimrog's head was temporarily obscured by a halo of steam.

Inspiration struck Kevin then. While Jimrog was distracted, he rushed to the balloon station. There was a heavy canister of gas. It wasn't just helium in that canister. Kevin knew it'd be hard to use as a weapon, but maybe he could get Jimrog to smash into it and blow both the cannister and Jimrog back to hell.

Kevin felt Jimrog more than saw him. The tile cracked beneath the weight of the beast. Kevin lunged past the cannister.

Jimrog swatted at Kevin and his hand slammed directly into the cannister. It was hard enough to crack the steel. The cannister exploded outward. Steel shard flew throughout the restaurant. Kevin cried out in pain. A piece had flown into his calf.

Kevin struggled to get away. He still had the mop, so he used that to pull himself away from Jimrog. He gingerly rolled over, making sure not to bump the steel sticking out of his leg. The beast was no where to be seen.

Jim was there though. He had been blown back into the scammy claw machine game. He was inside the prize area. He was bent in half with his butt firmly seated.

Kevin couldn't hear much of anything over the buzz in his ears. But he did see drops of blood falling onto the floor. He glanced about. There were a few people laying in their own blood too. He wasn't the only one hurt. Kevin fell back to the floor. He dropped the mop leaving bloody streaks behind.

Marrissa appeared next to him. She was saying something, but he couldn't hear her.

He was tired.

Then he saw something out of the corner of his eye.

He glanced over. The state police were spilling into the destroyed entrance.

"Fuck."

Dear Prudence

Dear Prudence,

I was at my wits end with him. I was exhausted by his mood swings, his irritability, unwillingness to listen, and just the fact that he would suddenly turn into a giant toddler.

So, I've been seeing this guy for about a year now. Most of the time, things are great. He takes me out to dinner, we go dancing, we have similar tastes in music and movies. Even if he doesn't like a specific musician or act the way I do, he certainly tolerates or indulges me.

It's just sometimes, with no explanation, he'll suddenly transform into a giant toddler. No, I mean, literally. He'll be himself, this tall strapping man, with an amazing beard. Then seconds later, there will be an actual 7 foot tall toddler stomping around, crying, and punching people.

Most of the time it's when we're out that he turns into a toddler, but I've definitely noticed he turns into a teenager or occasionally a toddler while we're alone together at home.

I've even recorded these events and he refuses to see it. He apologizes for being a dick, but he doesn't believe that he literally turns into a child.

– Don't want to Mother a man

Dear Mother,

First of all, you do not have to mother anyone. You are not responsible for fixing anyone. It is your partner's responsibility to get the help that they need and if you decide that you do not want to be a part of your relationship, that is perfectly acceptable.

If you decide that you want to stay with him, then you need to make sure he takes care of himself, not you doing it for him. So, I would recommend two things, first, is during one of the good times, suggest therapy. There are definitely occasions where men will turn into teenagers or toddlers when therapy is suggested. However, it will help them understand what's happening so they can take the next steps. In your man-child's case, you may be dealing with food allergies or some other reaction to specific foods.

I had a friend, he would turn into a moody teen every time he had gluten. If you put him around bright lights and/or loud noises, like at a concert, he'd almost always turn into a toddler.

Your friend may be experiencing the same thing. Now, this is why therapy is so important. removing things like gluten from the diet is a loss. It's hard to image a man without a beer in his hand, especially if they brew beer. Then he'll turn into a toddler because he has to confront his own mortality. That he's not a super human.

Between therapy and addressing these issues, I think you'll be on the right path. As an added bonus, all the pain he's caused in your relationship will be excellent fodder for him to discuss with his therapist or a couple's therapist!

Best of luck,

Pru

The Trial of Xyv$2)!^hq (Bob)

"All rise for the Honorable Judge Gregor Samsa," The bailiff cried.

Judge Samsa gestured for the defendant and gallery to be seated. The bailiff continued, "This is docket number One Nine One Five. State of New York vs. X-y-v-$-2-)-!-^-h-q, is that correct, sir?" The bailiff asked the defendant.

Deep within a cowl of darkness rumbled, "Close enough. However, if it is easier on your human throat, please call me Bob."

I glanced over at my client. It was difficult to make out much of anything of the ancient being. I could feel a pressure emanating from him. The easiest way to describe that, is that it's like something's hot that pressure you feel before you touch a hot piece of metal.

It'd been a tough six months working with "Bob" getting ready for trial. Bob knew so much, but only painted in broad strokes. If Bob just was blunt with me his defense would be much easier.

I turned my focus back to the rituals of the court. Trappings of legitimacy. Something for the Judge to hang his black robe on, not much to hang a man on, though.

The Prosecution was about to start his opening statement. I expected it to be a long one. It wasn't. Clearly, he felt this was an open and shut case. I shook my head.

After lunch, I began my opening statements. "I will be as brief as possible. This isn't about who my client is. Bob is who Bob is. An ancient being that's willingly binding Bobself into the rules of this court. Bob isn't truly bound by our courts, but has agreed to in this case. You are not to determine if a being so ancient is generally good or evil. Bob's power is difficult for humans to comprehend, however, that does not mean that Bob's power drives men 'Mad' as the prosecution has claimed. Or more exactly, caused a psychotic break in Officer O'Brien.

"That is all you are to judge Bob on. Did Bob's mere presence cause a man to have a psychotic break, wherein O'Brien killed a fellow officer and a bystander.

"I will show, that O'Brien exploited the fact that Bob appeared to murder Officer Freeman and Betty Freeman. That any further psychosis was O'Brien's and his alone. Bob did not trigger a new psychosis in O'Brien.

"O'Brien was a documented bigot and I have evidence that O'Brien was a member of the III%. The Freemans' were murdered in cold blood. Bob is a victim here. Thank you."

I sat. Shaking. It was a tricky defense, but the one Bob believed would work out best. Never ignore the fact that Bob was an ancient being beyond our comprehension.

I felt Bob's miasma wash over me. It was omnipresent in the courtroom, but sitting so close to Bob, it was suffocating.

"Excellent." I grimaced in pain as Bob's voice tore into my brain.

"Inside voices." I gasped. A drop of sweat hit my legal pad. The yellow paper hungerly sucked up the moisture. Creating an odd ripple.

The judge gestured to the state, "You may begin."

The Prosecutor, Javiar Char, began his case with the psych who treated O'Brien.

"What were your findings when you interviewed O'Brien?" Char asked.

"A man that had looked into the abyss and found it staring back. Found a monster, a horror. Something so beyond his comprehension that his mind broke. O'Brien continually repeated a phrase, 'Death is Growth' which we've all come to understand is a tenent in Bobism.

"After my evaluation, I found that Officer O'Brien's mental state would swing wildly. He was unable to sleep. He was chronically constipated, which is a common symptom of psychosis. He did not remember any of the events that lead to the Freemans' death."

"Do you believe that Eldritch Horror -"

"Objection! leading the witness."

"Sustained."

"What is your understanding of the cause of the psychotic break?" Char asks.

"Undeniably, the being sitting there." The shrink pointed at Bob.

"Your witness." char stated smugly.

"Sir, are you aware of the three other psychotic breaks O'Brien had?" I ask.

"No, what breaks are those?" He asks, voice shaking.

"Did you not get a full case history from O'Brien's psychiatrist? Well, please review these, here and here." I hand the man a folio.

After a few moment study, he looks at me, face white. "He, ah, murdered his wife while having another psychotic break."

"Just to clarify, you mean, O'Brien, right?" I ask.

"Yes." He cleared his throat. "He was on incredibly strong medicine at the time of this break. He'd never had a reaction like that on the drug. It is still firmly my opinion that only a being like Bob, that eldritch horror, could have caused another break in O'Brien."

"We will be sending your testimony and these cases to the NY State medical review board. Do you think they will be interested in your behavior here?"

"No, I did nothing wrong."

"You didn't do anything wrong by not fully investigating the history of your patient?"

"No. Yes, it was an oversight. O'Brien had withheld that information from me."

"Does O'Brien withholding that information change how reliable of a patient he was in your treatment?"

"He was an unreliable patient, as most patients with psychotic breaks tend to be. However, fully believe that we managed to get to the root of the issue with O'Brien. He fully believes he heard Bob's voice in his head."

"Does that mean a person had a psychotic break? Hearing a voice from Bob? A being that only speaks through telepathy?"

"What?"

"Yes, Bob only speaks to me through my mind. After my opening statement, he said 'Excellent' to me."

The therapist looked rattled. "I. Hmm, No, you are not having a psychotic break. O'Brien fit many of the other patterns."

"Do you believe any of his symptoms could have been coached? When he had murdered his wife, there was a great deal of skepticism at the time."

"I would need to spend more time reviewing that aspect of his history. I do not believe he was coached."

"You don't know though. No further questions."

The Prosecution called O'Brien to the stand. A thin hunched man, with long thin hair shuffled to the stand.

"Officer O'Brien, are you on permanent medical leave?" Char queried.

"Yes. My life has been a living nightmare. I am due on trial for the murder of the Freemans, though I'm not sure if I'll be competent to stand trial." the corner of his mouth quirked up.

"I object to this witness. Based on the previous witness, our evaluation, and the court's elevation, this witness isn't competent!" I cried.

Judge Samsa nodded his head, "I understand your concern. Despite the prejudicial nature of this witness, we believe O'Brien needs to answer questions in the name of justice. Overruled."

I leaned close to Bob, stars burst in my eyes as I whispered, "That will certainly be grounds for appeal."

I feel Bob nod next to me. I see an image of me writing an appeal, where I specifically call out this objection. The rest of the vision is clouded and obscured.

I rubbed my eyes, bringing me back to the present. O'Brien was going on about the difference between this psychotic break and the last one. How it was as different in feeling as a beer and a glass of wine. That an expert in psychosis knows the difference between the types of each. When your psychosis radically shifts, you notice.

As D.A. Char left the witness for me, I was inspired, "Officer O'Brien. Isn't it true you were reprimanded for being drunk on the job?"

"Yes, it was for an undercover case though."

"Would you say you're an expert in beer then?"

"Yes. Before the Flying Saucer shut down, I had a plate on the wall."

"That's impressive! Over 300 different beers, right?"

"Yes, I had more than one plate, I was over a thousand!"

"To become an expert in psychotic breaks, with the fineness of palette of beer, do you need 300, a thousand breaks?"

O'Brien swallowed, "I - uh- don't understand."

"Did you not just testify that you were an expert of psychotic breaks, that you can tell the immediate difference between your normal breaks and the alleged break that my client gave you?"

"Yes, it was as different as wine." O'Brien replied bluntly.

"How many breaks did you have before to tell the difference between beer and wine and not an Imperial IPA and a Belgian Kriek?"

"I don't know."

"Why were you still on the force when you encountered my client?"

"I had a waiver. My union got me special permission."

"Wasn't part of that waiver that you had to have a set of experts watching you while on patrol? On this particular day, they where the Freemans, correct."

"Yes." O'Brien sobbed, "I had to have a fucking baby sitter. I had two of them. Fucking brass didn't trust me."

"How many complaints did you have against you?"

"I don't know. They were all retracted."

"You had 250 complaints. Including rape, murder, and beatings. Are we to believe they were all psychotic breaks?"

"Yes. They all were."

"Why did Officer Altman retire?"

O'Brien hesitated, glanced to Char.

"Answer the question," Judge Samsa said

"I don't know," O'Brien said.

"I would like to remind the witness they are under oath."

O'Brien glared daggers at me, "Fuck you. He was forced to retire. It was retire or be retired."

"Why?"

"He snitched on me. He's fine, now though."

"Why weren't you forced to retire for medical purposes? 250 psychotic breaks should have been enough to give you a nice pension, right?"

"I got fuckin' results! It's fucking pieces of shit like you that gum up the works. I stopped crime by gettin rid of the criminals. I tossed wanna be gang bangers behind bars. They were sent there to rot, cause they were bad apples."

"Like you?"

"Objection!"

"Withdrawn. No further questions."

The prosecution fumbled through a few other witnesses of the O'Brien psychotic break. However, they did not have much to offer. O'Brien had been the lynch pin.

After a few days of prosecution, It was finally my turn. "The defense calls Officer Altman."

After Altman had been sworn in, I began my questions, "Officer Altman, could you explain the circumstances you were forced to retire?"

"Sure, I had filed a half dozen complains to Internal Affairs about O'Brien. Our leadership had enough of the complaints and brought in some of the union leadership, which was a clear violation of union rules, to intimidate me. I resisted for a long time, because I wanted justice for the women he hurt. Primarily prostitutes he'd raped, stolen drugs from, beat, etc... He had started to move on to victims and other perps. Apparently, NYPD leadership liked the results he was getting and wanted to turn a blind eye to the things he was doing."

"What about these claims of psychosis?"

Altman laughed, "Oh, yea, those claims. Look, before becoming a cop, O'Brien had been a licensed therapist. He worked at an office that treated patients with psychosis. He knew what it looked like. He knew how to lie about it." Altman snorted, "Do you know why he became a cop? Revenge. His brother had been killed in a drug deal gone wrong. So, he got into police work to take out whoever he thought was bad. If he got caught, he just pretended he was having a psychotic break or whatever. Everyone knew it was bullshit. Everyone knew he was exploiting the system. No one cared."

"I submit into evidence the multiple case files, the complaints, and O'Brien's therapy license and brother's case report. Tell me about his wife."

Altman sighed, "I was the responding officer to his wife's killing. She had filed for divorce. Somehow that had never gotten followed up on. On top of that her lawyer suddenly stopped talking to me. He failed to show up for a court date or whatever, so it wasn't included in the report. She had left O'Brien for his old therapy partner, a woman. O'Brien couldn't handle it and killed her. He was angry, but not psychotic when we got there. He knew exactly what he'd done and why."

"Was he left on the streets after that because he got results?"

"Objection, asks for speculation."

"Sustained" Judge Samsa replied.

"Nothing further." I stated.

D.A. Char stood up, "Isn't it true you had an NDA in place preventing you from discussing this?"

"Yes. I felt like I had a gun to my head, so I signed."

"Are you getting paid for this?"

"No, I might lose that pension I had been getting. The union is suing me."

"Is the defense representing you?"

"I wish." Altman sighed.

"Why did you have it out for O'Brien?" Char tried to change tact.

"A bad apple spoils the barrel. I was loosing credibility with my contacts because he was my partner. Hell, victims needed my protection from O'Brien. Mind you, that's victims of other crimes."

Char looked at his notepad. He sighed, "No further questions."

I glanced up at Bob, "Are you sure about this? You can continue to be silent. It's the best choice."

I squinted through the pain as Bob responded, "It does not lead to the desired outcome."

I stood, "The Defense calls Bob, the Defendant, to the stand."

"Tell me about the day you met O'Brien." I directed Bob.

Bob spoke, not in our mind, but with his voice. It was multiple overlapping discordant voices, like an out of sync and tune choir, "I met O'Brien on the first day I appeared in this universe. I had felt pulled to this dimension for some time, but did not feel it warranted my attention. However, as you humans began to create systems of economics, politics, justice, and many more, it became more interesting. So, I arrived at a scene of injustice in progress."

"Why did that matter?" I asked.

Bob's voice grated with effort, as Bob spoke the choir became a single voice, "I feed off injustice, death, and systemic failure. O'Brien was abusing a potential suspect. It was a delicious snack. However, to O'Brien I suddenly became a witness to him abusing someone. He lashed out at me. Of course, your weapons do nothing to me.

"The Freemans saw his impotence. Saw his terror. For, I looked more like this." Bob dropped his cloak of darkness. He turned into a riot of motion. O'Brien's report had described Bob has the Flying Spaghetti monster meets Cthulu, and it seemed pretty accurate.

The single voice continued, it was calm, soothing, "The Freemans cried out in terror at me. I made no movement. The man on the ground screamed for help. The woman, I believe, ran to the man on the ground, pulling him up. I stayed motionless. I believe at that time Officer Freeman assessed that I wasn't a threat and began questioning O'Brien about what was going on.

"O'Brien did not take kindly to that. He glanced at me, smiled, then turned back to Freeman and shot him. Then shot Ms. Freeman and the other man she was taking care of."

"What was that like seeing those murders?"

"Disgusting. The injustice in your justice system is gross. In both volume and consistency. It is like eating all the fried foods at the Texas State Fair. Yes, I grow fat and swollen from it, but it is not a healthy fat. It will doom me. And you."

"Why would you come here, then?"

The voices shattered into a chorus again, "The futures offered by humanity are fascinating. I can see many where humans resolve these issues and become a cross dimensional force for justice. I see others" a truly horrific voice dominated, "where humans become a cross dimensional force for injustice cloaked in justice. I am a fat swollen monstrosity in those futures, sickly and gorged on the vileness of humanity." A clear achingly beautiful voice dominates, "I prefer the other futures. I'm fit full, and happy."

"Why not abandon us and feed elsewhere?"

"No where will be safe from humanity, if you manage to survive the next few decades. Depending on how you survive is what matters."

"So, it's selfish?"

"Only partially."

"Did you directly attack O'Brien?" I ask, bringing the subject to the matter at hand.

"No. I did not directly interact with O'Brien, except when he shot me. I did not speak with him."

"No further questions."

DA Char stood, "Did you make him afraid?"

"He feared me. I did not force him to fear me."

"Do you know what questions I will ask you?"

"Yes. I also know various outcomes from the questions."

"Why are you going through this process?" Char asked.

"Because Justice matters. Cosmically, we must bend the universe towards justice. It doesn't happen on its own. Generally, entropy and injustice increase hand in hand. Being part of this process reduces injustice."

"How?" Char was curious, it seemed.

"By shining a light on the injustices of O'Brien, your police force, your office, and the prison system. Did you know three prisoners have died in your custody because of indifference, during this trial? They are wards of the state. You left them there to rot. All three were innocent. You could have let them leave at any time."

"Me?"

"You were their prosecutor. All three had been arrested by O'Brien after he murdered the Freemans."

Char suddenly fell to the floor. He began to writhe. He clawed at his face. He sat, looking dazed. Blood was oozing down his face, tears of blood spilled down his cheeks.

The bailiff rushed to the DA's side. "Are you alright sir?"

The DA gave the bailiff a confused look then straightened his tie. "Yes. I, was given a view of some of those visions. Bob, did you give those visions to anyone else?"

"Only the Judge and you."

"You need to give that vision to the Jury and anyone witnessing this trial. Because that is how our system works."

The court room filled with moans. I had already seen these visions, so they were not very surprising to me.

"The witness will not provide another vision like that without announcing the intent to do so. Is that clear." Judge Samsa admonished.

"Yes sir."

"Is the prosecution fit to continue?"

"I have no further questions."

"Defense Rests." I said.

"Motion to dismiss," Char said suddenly.

"Denied. Closing statements, tomorrow."

Char didn't show for closing statements. His second was required to give the statement. He, was unprepared.

I didn't have much to say, but to say that O'Brien exploited the situation and Bob wanted justice, despite feeding on injustice.

The jury returned within an hour. Bob was acquitted.

Bob shook my hand, the clear voice spoke, "We're starting towards a better path. Good work."

Dragon's War

Cyrus's stomach was in his throat. He could barely keep down his lunch. Even after 50 years, Lilly, his Dragon, still managed to find new ways to shock Cyrus with her maneuverability.

Cyrus glanced up at the passing matte black dragon. Its own rider struggling to stay mounted. As they leveled out, Cyrus pulled his bow, aimed and loosed his arrow. The black dragon flew its rider directly into the arrow. The rider bounced down the dragon's back pinwheeling into the clouds below.

Cyrus smiled at the surprised movement of the other dragon. He could see the widening of the eyes and the hitch in the wings. The dragon shifted its shoulders and then performed a flip that would have knocked a rider out. It just wasn't something a person could stay conscious for. The dragon darted down away from Cyrus and Lilly.

Cyrus could feel Lilly sigh in relief below him. That dragon had its sights set on her. Cyrus shook his head. What bad blood was there between them, he wondered. This was the 1328th year of the war. Lilly had been Cyrus's second dragon and he'd been flying with her for almost 40 years. This black dragon had been gunning for her every time they went out to fight.

Cyrus shook his head giving his bow a long look. This fight was never going to end, unless something changed. 1300 years is a long time. When the dragons first found this world, knights and swordsman ruled this world. The rest of the world moved on, though. Science dominated the rest of the world.

Cyrus was tired of that matte black dragon. He knew it'd be back soon. He pulled out the rifle from his bag. Lilly didn't know he'd brought it. Dragon's, generally, didn't like the weapons. They refused to fight if their riders brought them into the battle. Besides, the rifles couldn't hurt the dragons.

There. That black form. He saw it in his sleep. Cyrus would recognize the form of the wings in any sky. Of course, it was flying towards Lilly.

Cyrus took aim. He judged the wind and the speed of Matte, as he liked to call the Dragon. He pulled the trigger.

Cyrus held his breath. Lilly bucked under him. She screamed in his mind, "Why the fuck did you bring a gun, you ass?"

Cyrus did his best to keep his eye on Matte. The shot hit its mark. Cyrus saw a spurt through the dragon's head. It dropped from the sky.

Lilly cried in horror, "What have you done?"

"That dragon will never chase you again." Cyrus responded. He smiled, "Let's go turn the tide of this war and push those bastards back."

Cyrus felt his stomach lurch. Lilly was turning away from the battle. Cyrus's vision blurred, then narrowed. He struggled to keep it from going fully black.

She clearly planned on him passing out. She cried to the other dragons, "General retreat. General Retreat! The Fallen's greatest warrior, Black Mort, is dead." He could feel Lilly shudder, "My mate is dead."

Cyrus blinked, trying to maintain consciousness. He failed as Lilly continued to accelerate.

Cyrus found himself in the great hall. His great hall. The great hall his ancestors built to house humans and dragons. It was the warroom. The dining room. It was a place of feasts and mourning.

Cyrus's gun was on raised platform where he and his most important guests sat during feasts. However, he was not at the table. Trihorn was lording over the great hall. He was glaring at Cyrus.

Cyrus tried to shift in his chair only to find he was bound. He glanced about the hall finding dozens of humans and dragons about. There was clearly a divide between most of the humans and the dragons.

"Why am I bound in my own hall?" Cyrus called at Trihorn. "Who are you to usurp a human in their own home?"

Trihorn snorted, he intentionally released smoke. These dragons didn't actually breath fire or smoke, at all. They had decided to emulate the legendary dragons of Cyrus's people. Trihorn thought his magical smoke would somehow intimidate Cyrus. "You killed one of ours with this." The foreleg gestured towards the rifle. "You know these weapons are forbidden in the Great War."

Cyrus snorted, "Is that because this war is a war between family members? That I killed Lilly's mate? That you don't want other Dragons killed?"

"HOW DID YOU MAKE A GUN KILL A DRAGON?" Trihorn roared.

Cyrus shrugged, "I'm a smith. I learned long ago how to reforge arrows. The arrows that YOU want us to use on the other riders. Arrows that will barely hurt a dragon. Even if we aim perfectly."

Trihorn scoffed, "No arrows damage us."

Cyrus looked to his left, "Damian, your bow, shoot Trihorn with one of my arrows."

Damian started, "What my lord? Attack the great Trihorn? He is our ally."

Cyrus shrugged, "It is no matter, you will do no damage to him."

Trihorn gave Damian an inviting gesture. Damian shrugged. He quickly strung his bow and pulled one of his arrows. The arrowhead bore the mark of Cyrus's family. He drew the bowstring to his ear, straining with the effort. He took a moment to aim, "I'm aiming for your right foreleg's bicep."

Trihorn seemed to hold his breath, suddenly anxious. When the arrow loosed a moment of fear crossed the dragon's face. That flash turned into a cry of pain. Trihorn quickly pulled out the arrow and flung it to the ground. He rounded on Damian, ready to attack.

Lilly stepped forward, "Stop my lord. You ordered us to provide metal imbued with just a bit of magic to put a dragon out of the war for a day or two. This must be of that metal."

"It is Trihorn. I took that metal and made the gun and bullets that are before you." Cyrus coughed after yelling so loudly. "I wanted the matte black dragon to leave Lilly alone. Day after day, year after year, decade after decade, probably from the start of the war, Matte pursued Lilly. It was enough. That dragon had to die. We need this war to end. Generations of humans have died fighting this war. I'm almost 70. I have another 60 years to live, I don't want to die while we're still at war. This can end it."

Trihorn lunged down and tried to bite the gun in half. The great hall echoed with the sound of dragon teeth shattering. The great dragon reared back in pain flinging the gun towards Cyrus.

General Bronze cried, "We must put this trial on hold for now. The Judge is seriously injured."

"What trial?!" cried King Foolery. "This was a hearing to discuss this weapon. I never agreed to a trial. What are you trying Lord Cyrus for?"

"Murder." Bronze replied.

Foolery burst into laughter. His men hesitantly joined in. "Murder?" the King asked incredulous. "Boy, this is war. There is no murder in war. We've killed dragons in the past. Some of your kin have fallen to those dragons and their riders. Never before had you held a trial."

General Bronze scowled, "Dragons have been held for murder before."

The king straighten, "On both sides?"

"Yes."

"Never once has anyone held account for our deaths, yet you tell me you've held your people for murder of the enemy? Of the invading dragons? We are no less deserving of the same treatment."

Trihorn started to laugh. It sounded of bone grating on metal. It set Cyrus's teeth on edge. He noticed some of the men had moved closer to him.

Trihorn responded to the King, "Of course your lives aren't as deserving as ours. Your man there, Cyrus, I think, said he was going to live to 130." Trihorn laughed, "130? can you believe that there would be value in a life so short? Surely not. I will live to be 10,000 years old at the minimum. How can someone with such a short life span be considered worth while?"

Cyrus felt the ropes drop. He heard a number of the dragons gasp at Trihorn's statement. There was a general hubbub as the dragons spoke over each other. A few speaking in agreement most crying that this was the whole point of the war.

Cyrus lurched to his feet and dove for his gun. He took aim at Trihorn. He pulled the trigger before the large dragon could act. The bullet went straight through the center horn and out the back of Trihorn's skull.

Cyrus spit, "I hope you were already 10,000 years old."

Trihorn's body crashed to the floor. Silence settled over the hall. Lilly gasped, "What have you done?"

Strange Traveler

I felt my cart roll to a stop. The gravel crunched beneath the hooves of my mule. It was a dumb brutish animal and didn't like stopping only moderately less than starting again. It was an animal that liked things to be consistent. I tried to understand why the mule had stopped. We were on a straight section of road. Which in a high desert isn't hard to have. This plateau was an arid, hot scrub land.

I shook the reins, but the dumb animal didn't move. It snorted, SNORTED at me.

I muttered to myself in Ellean. The curse words sounded the most guttural in that language. The mule hated the sound of that language. The last owner only spoke Ellean. He had mistreated the mule. Likely giving it the foul temper it had. The mule was giving me a look then jutted its large chin down at the road.

Ok. the mule wasn't dumb. It was easy to call the animal dumb when it did unexpected things.

I sighed. I shuffled to the side of the cart and looked on the ground. There was a man laying across the road. Where the mule stopped, the only way to get passed would require moving the man.

I jumped down. If i'm honest with himself, and I'm working on that! It was more of a series of steps down. I'm getting older and my knees aren't very good any more. It's the wine barrels. They're heavy and don't move on their own.

After getting down I walked to the man. He was pale, paler than he would be if he was a local.

I surveyed the area. The road ahead didn't look recently used. I had seen no traffic in the past two days of travel. This plateau was scarcely traveled. I only took it because it was the fastest route from my vineyard to Mont Temtron, the closest village with relatively fast transportation to Kingsmont west of here.

There were no tracks leading from either direction of the road. It's almost like the man had just appeared here.

His lips were cracked. Despite my observation that he was pale, he was still rather red faced. The top of his head was actually beginning to bubble from the sunburn there. He was missing most of his hair. The top of his head was entirely bald. The sides of his head was cut fairly short and was a mixture of dark brown and gray.

His clothing was clearly foreign. My own being light colored wraps that covered nearly my entire body, but lose enough to let air pass through. My cart had a number of layers of cover, that allowed air to pass easy through, each layer was cooler than the last.

In the short time I had been on the road, I had already begun to perspire. I looked to the mule. I pulled an apple out of my shirt and let the animal chew on it. This time it only grazed my skin, rather than biting me firmly, like it had when I first started this journey. I think we were starting to come to an understanding.

I looked at the man. I kicked his boot. He didn't move. I squatted, well, I tried to squat, my knee didn't really let me squat, so I ended up half kneeling and half squatting to get closer to the man.

Dust was moving from around his mouth, so he wasn't dead, yet. I touched his skin. It was hot and dry. A bad sign. He was already dehydrated.

I picked him up. He was shockingly heavy. But then bodies always are. I managed to get him over one shoulder, like a farmer carrying a sack of roots. I shuffled myself around to the back of the cart. There, I lowered the gate and managed to shift him into the cart. I pushed him between some of the barrels to the coolest part of the cart. It was a solid 20 degrees cooler there.

Once he was there, I dripped some water into his mouth. Then I wetted a rag and let that slowly drip into his mouth. I made sure he could breath. Then I continued on my way.

Ok, that's not completely true. I did search him, see, here's his knife. It's really unique, isn't it? He let me keep it when we got to Mont Temtron. I did save his life after all.

I had another day on the road before getting to Mont Temtron, so it was really touch and go if he'd make it there, at all. The mule was excited that I had saved the man. It gave me a look that let me know it was pleased.

As I got back into my seat I glanced at the sun. It was going to be at its zenith soon. I knew I'd need to stop to protect the mule soon, but I wanted to get a little bit farther.

As the mule was continuing down the road. I studied the man more closely. he had a thin beard, like it was only a week or so old. It also looked like he didn't know how to care for it, even at his age. I could already see the beard was getting damaged. I felt bad for the man, not taking care of his beard. Not covering his head. It drove me to shake my head.

I looked at his clothing. They were of a style I've never seen before. They looked to be from a very far off nation. No one in Kingsmont would dare wear such a thing. He wore blue trousers of some kind with a simple belt. His shirt was a light green with a row of buttons going down the center like this. He had a jacket of some sort, but it looked more decorative than functional. It only had two buttons and left most of his chest exposed.

I noticed there was a cloth in the left breast pocket, I turned it into a bandanna to cover his head.

As I was administrating to his head, he suddenly cried out. Now, I know I had been very careful. He was not crying out about me.

He cried in a language I'd never heard before. He looked at me and cried in fright. I held out his cloth square bandanna. He gave me a look, one of pure malice and untied the knot and folded it back up. The entire time he was yelling at me. Almost like he was demanding something from me.

When he went into a coughing fit, which I knew he would, being that dehydrated and all, I gave him a small bit of water. He drank that greedily and tried to grab for more. I sighed and pulled it away.

I could tell I couldn't trust him alone, even with my trusty mule leading us down the road. I quickly scanned the immediate surroundings and noticed a small clump of shrubs with one tree. There might be some water there.

I leaned over and told the mule to go there. It nodded and directed the cart over that direction. It knew rest and water was coming.

The man was still yammering at me. His language wasn't nearly as gutteral as Ellean, but it was a fairly harsh sounding language. It sounded like none I'd heard before, so I cast a simple translation spell. You know the one, it takes what you've heard and lets you understand things and lets you speak back. Yep. He nearly jumped out of his clothes when I responded back in his language. I'm sure it wasn't perfect, but it was good enough.

I told him to calm down and if he drinks any more water he'd retch and be in an even worse state.

The Mule had gotten us to the little clump. I could see its smile. I told the man to wait in my seat. I told the mule to ignore the man so it could get food and water. It nodded.

The man did his best to get the mule walking again, but as I said before. Its a stubborn mule. I got the mule settled. I extended my covering. I created some water for the mule to drink in a rock trough. I could see how happy that made the mule. I'm glad, because I'd hate for that mule to try to kill me.

The man was spitting mad. He was crying about not being able to feel a Jesus or something like that. Jesus is apparently his god, or the son of his god, but also the same god. It's a bit like when one of us become an avatar for our gods.

I guess this man was a priest or something. He kept asking me what year it was, but never liked my answer of 2321. He claimed it was only 1995. I laughed at him. I told him he couldn't be from 1995, because the gods were warring on this plateau then. I pointed to the broken summit of Mont Fury, I tried to explain that Cassias, the god of Greed, had been shattered on that mountain top by Zewn, god of gift. You can still see Cassias's ribs if you're closer to Mont Fury. The god died there. Sadly, greed didn't die with Cassias.

He fell into a black silence then. It was nice. I was able to reflect on what he had been saying. Something about the United States, whatever that is, and that he needed to get back, they were in the middle of an election.

I gave him some more water slowly. He eventually slept. I made sure the mule was comfortable. We'd start out again when Mob flew from the sky.

I dozed for a while. The man had no weapons and was no threat to me. I woke to the sound of him retching. He was vomiting water. I simply rolled over and got some more rest.

A short while later he shook me awake.

"I can't feel him," He said over and over again.

"Your god?" I asked

"Right, I can't feel him," He sounded desperate.

"Are you sure you're on your world. Maybe your god isn't on this world. Maybe you're alone," I replied, annoyed.

"What country is this?"

"This is the landless land. No one dares claim this. Who would be so foolish to claim the battle ground of the gods. Their wrath would be unimaginable. We dare not call it anything but the plateau."

He squinted at me then. "I've never seen anyone that looks like you."

"Me? I'm not so uncommon. This blue skin is common in this part of the world." I gestured towards the sky, "Mob is very harsh here, Mob is smaller in Kingsmont. The blue gives me strength when Mob is large. My black eyes allow me to see in brightest of days up here. My beard helps filter out the dust storms." I pointed at him, "You are very uncommon here. I've seen people that look like you before, well, sort of like you, you're pinker than they ever were." I laughed then. He didn't like that.

"I'm American!"

"Hi american. I am called "Rufly. I hope you will survive the trip to Mont Temtron. Get some rest. Sip some water. I need rest."

After giving him a small sip of water, I rested again.

While I slept he had taken this large black block. He had pulled a large stick out from the back of the block. He was frantically pushing at button things on the block. Then he would cry in frustration.

"Why isn't anyone answering?" He cried in anguish

I glanced more closely at the block,"Does that allow you speak with people not here?"

"Yes, it's a Satellite phone. It uses things in space to call people in other parts of the world."

"Hmm. I don't understand any of that. Maybe call your Jesus. Maybe he can help you," I said helpfully.

He scoffed at me then, "Jesus only speaks to you when you pray."

I scoffed back, then. "My gods answer when I speak to them in a fire. Come look."

I summoned Dyredir then. She wasn't thrilled to talk with me, but she is the goddess of knowledge and knows all. "Dyredir, this man claims he's from nearly 400 years ago, can you help us?"

She gave him one look and laughed at him, "You are from another world. You are not from the past. Did you only summon me to ask this obvious question?"

I shook my head an prepared to ask another question.

He interrupted. I am still stunned that he survived his impudence. He asked, "Can you help me get home?"

Instead of smiting him, she gave him a sad look. It was heart rending to see her reaction. I'd never seen a god filled with such grief. She looked a touch helpless too. "No, I cannot. None of us can. That is useless here. You will need to find a way to live here."

She was gone then. You all are here to honor her. That goat is for her. A god should never be helpless, hopeless, and grief-stricken.

Instead of wailing the man stared into the fire. He had an odd look of determination on his face.

He put the block down and went to sleep. It was then I realized, that he had a warriors build. It was hard to see before with the strange jacket and clothes and being passed out and all. Now I saw it. His jaw was set. His shoulder were large and square. The shirt was tight across his chest and arms.

In the waning of the daylight we awoke. He asked me if other lands had other gods. I told him yes. He nodded and asked if I would help him get to another land. I said I would. He nodded and didn't say another word for several hours.

As we got closer to Mont Temtron, he asked he for different clothing and a weapon. I told him I had no weapons, just my magic. I offered to heal him. He accepted that and my extra clothing.

The mule gave me a look. I sighed. I reached behind me an pulled out my well worn sword. I cast a spell and duplicated it. I gave the duplicate to the man, American.

He drew the sword and tested it. He must have been satisfied as he nodded and then rested again.

When we got to Mont Temtron, the man hugged me and thanked me for helping him get through his moment of crisis. That if he can, he will repay me for everything I'd done for him. I gave him back everything else I had taken from him. He let me keep this knife. I gave him some money and explained how to get to Kingsmont. I also gave him a necklace to learn languages faster.

Now, I'm back home. I have no idea how he's fairing.

Dyredir, I just hope I've pleased you with this story, goat, and company. I cry. I stare in shock as Dyredir comes full body out of the flame and consumes the goat. She turns and consumes my father in-law. I can't act. What can you do against a god?

Dyredir turns and faces me, "You. You are the reason there's a war in heaven. That man. He's trying to bring a new god into our pantheon. It's an angry god. One that's unwilling to share power. You must right this wrong."

Burnt Forest

Two small squirrel like animals were chasing each other. One happened to catch the other and they rolled across the gently sloping grass covered hill.

A mechanical hiss startled both animals from their frivolity. They darted away towards the nearest tree. The slower of the two barely making it out from under the edge of a heavy ramp. It was corrugated for easier purchase during bad weather evacs.

The animals chittered at the loud thing. It was a massive object. Brutal in its design. No consideration to form, function was the only aesthetic that mattered to its designer.

Shapes began to pour down the ramp. The beings had more in common with the thing they were leaving than the two animals watching.

Strange noises emanated from the area where a head should be. Instead of eyes, there were reflective black holes. Emotionless, soulless black stared back at the animals.

One of the thing walked towards the forest. It was several dozen trees away from the animals, so they watched with trepidation. A limb reached up behind the thing and pulled something from the back.

The thing pointed it at the trees. Fire leapt towards the tree. The thing was waving it back and forth across the trees.

The animals screamed.

One of the being's face voids turned towards the animals. The arms pointed in their general direction. Another being stepped forward. He reached behind him.

The two animals raced through the tress, away from the beings. Hoping to outrun the destruction. Hoping they could find someone or something to confront the things that destroyed their home.

A Retelling of Arthur's Story

Arthur stared at the throng of people. They were feting, dancing, cheering. Arthur's stomach growled. Most importantly, they were feasting. There was a banner over the whole thing. Supposedly it said something about the King's 40th birthday.

Arthur turned as another part of the seething mob let out a collective moan of disappointment.

"The young King Lancel just failed at removing the sword." Morgana whispered in his ear. Arthur turned to her. He started, as he almost always did at her eyes. They held an age and wisdom well beyond her 8 years of age. It was said Merlin's eyes were the same flickering and dancing hue.

Arthur grunted in return. He had another 9 months before he could give the sword a try. He wiped sweat from his eyes, "Let's steal some food."

Arthur watched the men struggle at the sword. They all hoped to pull the sword from the stone before the King returned. The aging king had been on a tour since his birthday 9 months ago. Today he'd be returning. The queue beside the stone was longer than it'd been since the King's birthday. Arthur was in that queue. He was finally 10. Old enough to try the sword.

Arthur hadn't tried to time his turn with the King's arrival. It just happened that way. The trumpets blared announcing his arrival through the gates. Arthur knelt, impatient to give the sword a pull.

The king reined in next to the group of men and women. "I see there's a grea many of you hoping to become heir upon my return.

Young man, you seem to be holding up the line. Go ahead, pull the sword out of the stone." These were the words the King always said when watching someone make an attempt.

Arthur didn't know that. He felt a heavy burden fall upon his shoulders. He stood, shoulders bowed. He shuffled to the sword. The larger men behind him snickered at the thin young man.

Arthur touched the sword. He felt it quiver. He started. The crowd laughed. "It's a sword not a snake. It won't bite you!" cried a voice from the mob.

Most of the crowd was focused on the boy. Morgana was staring intently at the King. He too had started when Arthur started. Like he felt some jolt.

Arthur adjusted his stance. He made sure he could pull the sword with a clean movement. He put both hands around the sword and pulled.

The sword pulled smoothly from the stone.

The sound was jarring, like two boulder grinding against each other. The crowd was silenced. Men were staring in awe.

Arthur staggered back. The sword tip crashed into the stone, sending sparks into the crowd.

The king called, "Boy, what is your name?"

Arthu stared back, mouth agape. Morgana answered for him. "My king, his name is Arthur. I am his sister, Morgana. I can vouch that his birthday is today and he is 10 years old."

"Well met Morgana." The King said. "All kneel before, Prince Arthur!" His voice boomed in the crowd's stunned silence.

The old King died only a few years later. Arthur was barely 15. News spread fast. King Lancel, the closest country and often at odds with Camelot, was the first to strike. Arthur, with the help from Merlin and his apprentice Morgana, swiftly defeated Lancel's main host capturing the king.

Arthur questioned him, "Why did you raise your hand against my people, while we still mourned?"

Lancel sneered, "You are destined to unite all of Britain. If the country is united under you, what happens to the other Kings?" Before Arthur could answer, Lancel continued, "No. I knew you were but a child. So, I struck, hoping to claim your sword and your throne and unite Britain myself."

Arthur pondered this. After three days of thought, he visited Lancel again. "What should happen to Kings when I unite Britain? Your people are now my people. If I kill you, then your people may rise up. If I imprison you, then your people may try to break you out. I will instead send you on a quest. You will help me fulfill another prophecy. You will seek the grail. You will search for 2 years before you return."

"If I refuse?" Lancel calmly asked.

"You will tell your people of your cowardice. That you refused to find the grial. The grail that ends illness, mind you. That for this cowardice, I will punish you to death." Arthur smiled as the man slowly blanched.

Lancel returned to find a very different Britian. He had heard rumors of wars in Britian. Where Kings had followed Lancel's lead and struck at Camelot. King's Galahad and Perceval had failed and were sent on the same quest as Lancel.

Lancel rode through his former country. His small retinue behind him. He'd managed to find some support abroad, mostly in Gaul, but not in Britain. His people were happy. He entered the village square of Bath and there were mid summer celebrations ongoing. The peasants were fat. They were dancing.

"Sir Lancelot!" Cried one of the peasants.

"I am your rightful King!" Lancel called, drawing his sword, "You shall treat me as such."

"Sorry my lord. But you are not." another peasant replied. A crowd started to gather.

"You are the first of the Kights of the Round Table." a priest had worked his way through the crowd. It was his former adviser Lionel. "Our people are happy under King Arthur's rule. You are part of that rule. You are a hero, searching for the very thing that will heal the only people Arthur cannot. The sick, the ill. What word do you bring?"

Lancel glanced about confused. The crowd's mood had quickly shifted, from happy, to angry, to hopeful in just a few words. He took a breath. "I have not found the grail yet. I came to giv word to Arthur of the status of my quest. I have tiding from the King of Gaul. I will continue my quest. To help my people."

The first peason called,"We know you will be successful, come! Let's celebrate. It's mid-Summer after all, my lord!"

Lancel met his King. "My Lord. I have met my people. They have prospered in my absense. I thank you for your care."

Arthur smiled, "Of course. Your people are my people. I heard you were greeted as a hero. I'm glad. What tidings do you have?"

Lancel's smile faded, "None. I was unable to find what I sought. I have failed, my king."

Arthur patted his arm, "You have not succeed, yet. That is all. You may need to go farther than Gaul. Jesus was in Israel, after all. Come, we must plan for battle. Your former ally, Gawain, is assaulting your people. It would be good for us to defend them, together."

Over time, Arthur and his Knights of the Round, all former liege lords of Britain, fully united Britain. Some Knights, such as Tristian elected to join the Kingdom of Camelot rather than join through force. Peace fell across Britian.

By the time Arthur was 40, the same age as the old King, peace had reigned for nearly a decade. Arthur's son, Morgoth, was hungry for glory.

"Father, I am 15, the same age you were, when you first conquered Lancelot. I beg you to let me earn my honor."

"Son, war is not the only way to gain honor. War of aggression, against the weak, against the helpless, is not an honorable war. Despite unifying Britain, I never once started a war with a neighbor." Arthur sighed.

Before Morgoth could reply, Gawain rushed into the hall. "My lord. The Gaul's gather for war."

"Why after all this time?" Arthur's brow bunched. His hands clenched his armrest.

"I shamed them. During my search for the Grail, I happened to be there, when a Green Knight challenged their knights. A single blow for a single blow. None would answer. I slew the knight. Or at least removed his head. He rose from his beheading and told me to find him in a year. Leaving his axe.

"A year later, myself and a number of the Gaulish knight found the Green Knight. I offer my head, unflinching. The knight decided not to take my head. He gave me his axe in honor of my bravery." Gawain removed an axe, that was both heavy and inspired by the forest.

"The Gauls took exception. They were embarrassed and incensed.

They took this as a stain on their honor and have declared to regain their honor through conquest."

Morgoth spoke, "There is no honor in war for war's sake."

Gawain appraised Morgoth, "You speak wisely, my prince. Britain is lucky to have you as heir."

Arthur cleared his throat, "We must prepare. The Gauls are a threat we mustn' under estimate."

The Gauls made landfall, pushing back the Arthur's defense. The Gaul made steady progress. Starting with Tristian's land first. Arthur held a war council. The knights in Britain were present, along with Merlin and Morgana.

Arthur, "We must hold. What can we do to hold these brutes back. Merlin, can you summon a fog to allow us to ambush them?"

Merlin shook his head. "I cannot. I can summon the rest of the knights to Britain. I have foreseen the only manner for victory is with a united Britain."

Arthur considered this. "Do it. We will hold until they have all returned. We will protect our people as well as we can." He turned to Morgoth, "You will lead a host with Lancel to protect our people. For a king is nothing without their people. Lancel, has experience with this and will teach you. Listen well."

"I should be leading the host in defense of our land. I need the honor of defending our land." Morgoth whine.

Arthur looked at him sharply, "The land is nothing without its people. You are defending Britain."

Morgoth sneered, "Come Lancel. Let us plan."

As the rest of the Knight left, Merlin leaned close. "That one will break the Unity of Britain unless something changes."

"What do you advice Merlin?" Arthur's shoulder sagged. He rubbed his eyes.

"Offer him something he wants. Perhaps, let him lead the fighting withdrawal."

"I will discuss with Lancel after this initial evacuation." Arthur waved away his adviser.

Arthur's knights trickled in. One by one. The fighting retreat gaining strength. Morgoth, though, was more and more sullen each day he was away from the front.

A Gaulish company snuck past the main lines and assaulted a village under Morgoth's command. His units responded immediately, removing the threat with minimal damage. Morgoth gave chase. Leading a flanking assault on the Gaulish forces. Lancel was mortally wounded in the battle.

Arthur met with Lancel on his deathbed, "My friend, I am shamed that we could not hold back the Gauls. That we could not push them back."

"My lord." Lancel coughed, "It is not your fault. Morgoth betrayed me. He struck me while I was locked in combat with a Gaulish commander."

Arthur gasped, "I have failed as a father." He wept. "Merlin warned me. I didn't listen."

Lancel shook his head, "You didn't fail alone. Put him on the front. Leave Gawain here. The front may deal with the problem."

Arthur stood, stunned. "I will have Merlin stop by."

Arthur paced the halls of Camelot. He did not sleep. Could not go to bed. He found himself in the kitchens as they started baking the bread for the day.

"My lord," cried a scullion. She cleared her throat and attempted a curtsy, "How may we help you?"

"Just some bread and watered wine." He murmured.

The young girl ran off. Arthur sat and stared at the battered work table. He could smell the flour. The yeast from the proofing bread.

The scullion returned putting a plate in front of her king. "Anything else my lord?"

"Just a question, if your child did something unforgiveable, what would you do?" The king ask quietly.

The girl gaped at him. "Um, ah." She cleared her throat. "I would send him away. Make him join the army. Nothing's so unforgiveable that saving our people can't make forgivable."

The king nodded. "Thank you dear. You may go. If your chef questions you send her to me." The girl quickly nodded and ran off.

Arthur slowly ate the bread. It was day old bread. He used the watered wine to soften it. It was almost as good as grape jam on the bread.

He dusted his hands off, stood, quaffed his wine and left the kitchen.

Later during their war council, "Morgoth. You will go to the front line. I will give you command of the eastern front. I will remain in command of the center. Gawain. Take over Lancel and Morgoth's command."

Gawain's face darkened. "I will do as you command, though I fear you are surrendering our eastern flank. There are rumors about Lancel's wounding." Gawain threw a dark look at Morgoth. "I will go meet my commanders."

Gawain swept out of the council before it's conclusion.

Morgoth beamed. Ignoring the discord he had sown.

Arthur sighed. He held his head. There was no good solution.

The eastern flank almost immediately collapsed. Gawain was sent in to relieve Morgoth. He solidified the flank. Morgoth was furious. He stormed into his father's solarium. "What is the meaning of this? You give me a command and immediately take it from me."

"You were to learn from Lancel. You learned nothing. The feint you fell for was obvious. Learn from Gawain. Once you can hold the eastern flank, you will lead the counter assault. You will counter conquer Gaul."

"NO" Morgoth screamed. Spittle landed on Arthur's boots.

"What do you mean, 'No'?" Arthur asked quietly.

"I will take over full command now." veins bulged on Morgoth's forehead. His face was red.

"Did you kill Lancel?" Arthur asked.

"You dare ask me that? You take his word over my own?" Morgoth stepped back. "You don't love me at all. How can my own father, dare to ask me that?"

"I see." Arthur stated. He sighed and stood. He walked towards a window, back turned to Morgoth. "I taught you everything I knew. I failed you, my son. It is not you, it's my failure as a father that made you who you are."

Arthur felt the icy blade in his back. He knew he was dead before he knife fully entered. Arthur pulled his own knife. He thrust backwards, into his son's chest.

Morgoth pushed Arthur forward, sending Arthur through the window. Morgoth staggered back. Knife embedded deep into his chest.

He touched the blade and retched. Morgoth fell to his knees and pulled the blade out. Blood poured out onto the floor. Staining the shape of Britian below him. He dropped the knife, it bounced and impaled Camelot.

120

Al The Flower Guy

I had just turned 15, when it happened. My mother was so excited, she exclaimed, "OH, look someone's getting their powers!"

My "powers" were so embarrassing. I could manifest flowers. That's it. They couldn't grow, they couldn't choke anyone. They didn't protect me. They were literally flowers. I could be the worlds greatest florist.

Let me take a step back. I'm the oldest son of the worlds most important, not powerful, but important hero. He runs the Powered School and a group of heroes called The Teachers. Dad, who goes by Silence, is a tactical genius as a solider. He wins not by brute strength, but by getting the most out of his people.

My mother is one of the most powerful people on that team. She can teleport, is invulnerable, super strong, you know god tier powers. She might not be able to fly, but when you can teleport the way she can, what's the difference? Her name? She just goes by Mother. Apparently, she had a different name, but she was so motherly to EVERYONE, they just called her Mother.

Everyone expected me, Al, son of Mother and Silence, to have some extraordinary set of powers. I was not gifted with super intelligence. I struggled in school. I was slow and unathletic. The only varsity team I was able to join was Heroes Unleashed, a team based video game. We won our state, New York, and got second in nationals. We're ranked for the upcoming Olympics and a serious contender for medaling.

The worst part of my powers manifesting is that I was celebrating winning States when they manifested. I was pumping my fists and high fiving when a bouquet of flowers appeared in my hands.

Everyone laughed, thought it was a magic trick. I wish it was. Mother, told me that some people uncover new powers over time. It's been 3 years. I'm going to be joining a pro gaming team as an alternate. Hopefully I'll be a starting team member soon.

I'm not able to join the Powered School, because there isn't anything worth teaching me. I'm a horrible failure. I will never live up to my parents. I'm an embarrassment to my friends. Most of my friends got awesome powers, like Tim, he can speak any language, hold a ton of conversations at once, and is a genius. He's already working as a diplomat and has negotiated peace deals between two countries that have been at war for decades. Then there Samantha, she's got God Tier level powers. She can fly, generate any material she wants with a single thought. She's trained herself to react with protective shields without thinking. She's already saved the space station and built huge add-ons. She just made more oxygen and water for them. She's building a base on Mars for astronauts to be greeted with.

I gave her a huge bouquet when she landed. She just looked embarrassed for me. I cried later that night. What else can I do? My friends don't even want to get flowers from me. It's like a reminder to them of my inadequacies. My failures as a hero.

Mother is supportive. Silence, though, isn't nearly as supportive. He looks at me with a mix of disappointment and shame. Like I'm a reflection of a failure within him. That he's at fault that I can only manifest flowers. He flies into rages when I give him flowers after a tough mission. Even if they are manly flowers.

Mother loves them. She often brags about how the flowers reflect my kind heart and suits me.

I think I keep giving these flowers to Silence to point out to him that this is his fault. That I should have different powers. I resent this. I didn't ask to be his son. I didn't ask for the expectations. The constant, "Can't wait to see what powers you're gonna have!" Then to manifest the ability to give flowers. It's pathetic.

Al signing off (August 3, '77)

Well, I actually stopped a bank robbery today. It was crazy and accidental and I got really lucky. I was depositing my pro gamer check, cause I got promoted (sorry! it's been a few weeks journal).

I normally deposit my checks through my phone, but this one exceeded my phone's limit, which is CRAZY.

So, I'm in the bank and I'm talking with the teller about where to put the money. She was a cutie so I gave her a flower. She blushed and put it into her jacket.

Just after doing that, The Nose burst into the bank. Now, the Nose, is well known for his ability to sniff out merchandise for his bosses. Of course, that would make him very sensitive to other smells.

He comes in guns drawn demanding access to the vault. That there's stolen merchandise in there that must be returned. Now, the Nose is very recognizable, because of his titular nose. So, I just created all sorts of foul smelling flowers. I completely buried him in them. To the point that he was tripping over the flowers.

He started to go into convulsions and the guards were able to apprehend him without anyone getting hurt.

Maybe there is some sort of use for this flower power. It also got me thinking, maybe I can just make the flower smell without needing to make the flower.

Al signing off (Sept 15, '77)

Well, I think I've made peace with who I am. A few days after the last entry, I was captured by Ms. Electric and Furball. They took me to Sir Dolton. Apparently Sir Dolton had hired the Nose. Long story short, my left hand was damaged to the point I will never game professionally again. I was saved by Silence, Mother, Tim, and Samantha. And of all people, The Nose.

How they found me was ingenious on my part. I created a very distinct odor that was almost unnoticeable, but was detectable by some of the tools the Powered School has. I started to create it as soon as Ms. Electric cornered me. I also dropped a bunch of petals with a similar scent, so they could link the two.

After being saved, I had to do some serious soul searching. It was hard. I went to therapy, I used a totally different journal, since I couldn't type. I talked with friends.

Samantha was getting married to Tim, she asked me for a special perfume. We spent days getting the perfect mixture of scents for her big day. I also did the flowers for the event with a great wedding coordinator.

As a result, I've decided to open a hyper exclusive perfume shop. I will match any sent or create a custom sent just for you. In a strange twist of fate, The Nose is going to be working for me in a work release program. Apparently, he really loves this sort of work.

I have made so many people happy with these perfumes. It's, kind of amazing. I guess you don't need to run around saving the world, to make it a better place.

Al signing off (December 31 '79)

Host: We are here with LaSean "The Nose" Hampton looking back at his time with Al "Perfume Artist" Lee. So, I understand that you met Al under some less than ideal circumstances.

LaSean: Heh, yea, less than ideal is an understatement. I was working for The Boss at the time. Now, I normally wouldn't take a job like this, but my wife had just given birth and we were strapped for cash. So, I was hired to acquire some goods. It turns out they were in a bank. I could smell them. I knew the bank would hand them over and get the insurance money. Well, Al buried me in Terrible! I mean, just the worst smelling flowers. They were the flowers that smelled like death. This was very embarrassing for me, as Al was a joke among the criminal underground.

Host: So, you're then offered the opportunity to find Al, when John "The Boss" Smith, kidnapped him. Tell me about that.

LaSean: Well, it was a pretty straight forward choice. Help Silence and Mother find their idiot and incompetent son or get 10-15 years for what I did. Not a hard call, right? [Laughs] Al, was pretty quick to figure out a way to leave a trail for us to follow. He left some very subtle but distinct smelling petals behind. Surprisingly, Furball didn't smell them. Her nose was very good, not as good as mine, but definitely top 10 noses at that time. Once I was taken to the scene, it only took the time to fly along his scent to find him. Mother was generous enough to carry me. [Laughs]

Host: Then you were put on a work release program.

LaSean: Yea, um. That was a doozey. After this kid helps arrest me, I save him, the state didn't think I should be done with him. They made me help him make exclusive perfume. He was stumbling along. He could make any smell you want, but if you wanted the exact same thing twice, he really struggled. So, we were put together. I hated it at first. This kid was so arrogant and wet behind the ears. On top of that he had a chip on his shoulder because he didn't get the powers he wanted. It was a tough couple years getting through our issues. He had a lot of growing up to do. What really sealed our friendship though, and this was while I was on work release, was a time he overheard me hear news that my trans cousin was missing. I lost my shit, er, mind. He pulled me aside and said that we got work to do. He said we needed to go deliver a new perfume to my missing cousin. She special ordered it while I was in lock up.

Host: had she?

LSean: No. he was lying, lying so we could go find her. Because of him, she's alive. He suggested that we create a custom perfume to give out to the at risks youths and minorities. A different sent for each group so we'd be able to help find them. We sold some of them to rich white folk, but almost all of it was given away for free. That was a turning point for me. I was convinced to keep doing what I was doing. I was able to help people. It helped Al a lot. Al was able to save people like them. It also turned Al's powers from something that was somewhat embarrassing into something really positive. Something that saved lives. Al kept a tracker of all the people it saved. All the people that were put to justice. Al, really felt like a hero because of that. Al was. I'm devastated Al's gone. The world is fouler without Al in it.

Coffee Assassin

I opened the door for her. She did have shockingly blue eyes as everyone said.

"Who the fuck are you?" She demanded, eyes blazing, literally.

"I've just put on the kettle. Let's have some coffee and talk."

"You're him! Aren't you?!" She didn't bother waiting for a reply. She shot lightening from her eyes.

I sighed. They all do this. "Come now. Stop this. Let's have some coffee."

"How? Where did..." She trailed off, terror filled her eyes. The spark didn't die though.

I gestured for her to take the lead. I follow her through her house. It's a nice open layout house. Her time as a hero turned villain has served her well. The foyer was large, the hallway to the kitchen had a great mix of paintings and pictures. Pictures with her former hero team and her current villainous partner.

I paused at one. It's her and a dead teammate. The two women are kissing. The woman's death supposedly triggered her flip from "good" to "evil."

"It's really true about you, then?" She asked.

I nodded in reply. Uncaring if she saw the gesture. "Please sit." I took the seat across from her. The kettle was on the counter behind me along with most of my coffee accoutrement. "I've been hired to kill you. However, I cannot simply kill a person. It goes against my code and abilities. I must judge you first. To do that I need to hear your story. We will go walk through a series of coffee types as you do. I've found this makes the process easier on you. If you are deemed worthy of death, at least you'll have gone out with something delicious on your tongue."

She set herself a stubborn glare, "I don't like coffee, though."

I gave her a quiet smile. I began to prepare the Aero Press. I set the pieces up and began to hand grind the beans.

Her eyes flashed. I shook my head as lightning arced from her eyes. I looked at the grinder. The beans were scorched and the burrs were slagged.

I went to my bag and pulled out another hand grinder. This one was rubberized and wouldn't succumb to her powers. She tried again, but the lightening was almost immediately grounded.

She groaned, "Fucking physics."

I was finally able get the grinds into the aeropress and go through the process of brewing the coffee.

After gently pressing the water through the filter, I slid a cup towards her. She stared at it pouting. Her arms were crossed, she glowered at the mug.

She sighed and picked up the mug. She let the steam envelope her. As she was doing so I began grinding a mug for myself.

She took a sip. I felt myself relax. I stretched my neck, felt a joint pop. She seemed to melt into her chair. She sighed again, but the tone and energy was so different. I felt the comfort she was feeling.

"This is delicious. Best coffee I've had, since... Since, Sarah was killed. She had won the World's Barista Competition a few years ago."

She glanced up at me, a tear at the edge of her eye, "It's funny, until I met her, I never thought much about baristas. Didn't even know that there was a competition for them. Coffee was just... coffee. Something that perked me up in the morning. She turned it into an event. When she made it at home, it was like a ritual." She wiped her cheek, that tear had become a river.

I gently pressed out my coffee.

"So, is this what you want? Some sort of last minute confession?" She demanded.

I took a sip of my coffee. It was very good. Maybe a little over extracted, but very excellent texture. I set down my mug and fixed her a look. "This is what you make of it. What do you choose to do with the last mug of coffee? What do you want me to know, what do you want me to let the world know?"

She sipped her coffee and stared out the kitchen window. "Why don't you kill every bad person out there? Why didn't you kill the Silver Jaguar before he killed my Sarah?"

"They didn't find a body," I whisper. "You know, I don't like doing this. I am very selective about my jobs. The Silver Jaguar? Pfft, almost any hero could have taken him out. Could have been arrested and tried a dozen times. He just wasn't important enough, compared to the Crimson Moon or Captain Bones. Besides, his story is well known. He turned out the way he did because of the system. Born in the wrong part of town to the wrong parents. Had the wrong color skin. Wrong types of powers." I shrug.

I gesture towards her with my mug, "Now you, you're different. You chose this. You're not someone any hero can go toe to toe with. Everyone assumes they know your story."

"That's what this is about? Collecting stories?" She asks, disgusted.

"Stories are the only thing we leave behind that last. A good story can outlast empires. The important question, though, does your story end here?"

"Fuck you!" She grabbed her mug and splashed coffee at my face. She lunged towards a knife.

I rewound. She blinked and glanced down at her mug. It was full of coffee. "What? How?"

"You could have stopped Jaguar! You could have saved Sarah! Why didn't you act!" She cried. She lunged towards the knives again.

I pulled the coffee in her stomach. She dropped to her knees clutching her gut. She glared at me, then glanced at the mug in horror.

"I'm already dead, aren't I?"

"On the one hand your death is a formality, yes, you're already dead. On the other hand, once your body processes the coffee you'll be fine. Drinking more at this point would only make the end faster, or delay being clear of it a bit slower. If you're alive after this, you'll never see me again, though."

She jammed her finger down her throat and began to retch. She threw up again and again. She sat in her chair, leaving a puddle of bile on the floor. She smiled at me, "I'm free from you now."

She shot lightening out of her eyes again. I rewound, slowly. I made it take a full minute, ensuring she experienced the full process. Lightening flew back into her eyes, she flopped from the chair to the floor. Vomit returned to her stomach, her finger pressed into her throat. She felt the coffee tear at her stomach again. Then found herself in the chair again.

She looked at me in horror. She looked down at her clothing, it was vomit free. She had thrown up into her hair, but it was dry.

"I've been dead since I walked in the door, haven't I?" she asked, voice quivering.

"Tell me your story."

"No."

"Ok. Would you like more coffee?"

"No."

"For what it's worth, I'm sorry. I loved you."

Recognition flashed across her eyes. I flicked my wrist and the blaze in her eyes was snuffed out. I cried, mourning her loss, again.

By the Gods, a Tournament

"Husband," she cried. "Why did you think, ahhh," she dodged a blow, "that a tournament of champions was a good idea?"

Her husband sent a bolt of lightening into a contestant. His eyes widened as the bolt was absorbed into the man. Her husband grinned.

"Leo! Are you listening?" She screamed. Fury in her eyes. Flames sprouted on her eyelashes. She fixed a look at the man attacking her. She grabbed him and crushed his skull. As his skull rapidly reformed, she screamed at him, "Just give me one second to talk with my husband, alright?" She whipped her hair back and grabbed the back of her husband's head and threw him into the ground.

"Leo, DO. I. HAVE. YOUR. ATTENTION?" She screamed into his ear. Blood oozed out almost immediately. "Fuck!" She yelled. A hazy energy based spear jutted from her abdomen. She pivoted and pushed the wielder. The wielder went flying.

She punched the ground, stunning or knocking most contestants over. "Give me five fucking minutes to talk to my idiot fucking husband. He concocted the whole damn thing."

She picked Leo up, "Send them back." She said quietly. "Now."

Leo looked at her half dazed, "Why? I've been planning this for years! Isn't it glorious?"

"I am glad our constant warring with the mortals had stopped."

"You said you were bored, my love." Leo said confused.

"You took that and did this?" Scorious scoffed. She threw him aside. "Deal with it." She called over her shoulder, "Or I'll deal with you."

* * *

She walked away and blinked away from the stadium. Leo watched her go. Her after image still seared in his eyes. He rubbed his eyes and snapped his fingers. The contestants vanished. Well, most of them. He concentrated on one after another, they all left. Except for one.

That one. He was powerful. He knew the arts and there was something different about him. He wasn't of Earth.

That one floated over to Leo. He was wearing silver and blue suit with golden accent. A bold symbol of red streaked across his chest. Leo glared at him as he approached.

The man, despite not being of Earth, really looked like he was from Earth, which was abnormal. Leo saw it then. He was from the future of Earth. Where humanity had changed so much they were nearly alien.

The man stopped,"You have a few options. You can never interfere on Earth again, especially like this. You can act and help protect the people of Earth. Or we will come back and destroy you and your people."

Leo scoffed, "We will do as we please. We are your gods."

The man appraised him. Minutes passed. He didn't flinch or look away when Leo looked him in the eye.

"What are gods that are unworthy of worship?" The man asked.

"You refer to the fallen. They reside, below."

The man laughed. He LAUGHED at Leo. Leo felt his anger boil he readied a blow as the man came closer. The man said, "Then go below. You the unworthy."

"Who do you think you are, judging me?".

"Some call me the Coffee Assassin. Most call me The Protector. I have judged you unworthy. Go below."

He rose up above the stadium, "All of you witness to this barbarity, know he has been judged unworthy. By his own words, an unworthy god must go below. It is your duty, your penance to see him go below.

"I will return. If he has not been sent to this other realm you all, will be judged. You have one Earth week." The Protector waited a moment, then vanished.

Scorious rubbed her eyes. The being was right. Most of the gods or immortals on this plane enjoyed the fight and happily joined in. None had lifted a hand to help the people on Earth in centuries.

Scorious glanced at the being most worshiped on Earth, Abra, they had a fractured appearance. Difference faces would rise to dominance. Each with a different personality. They had been inactive for several centuries. Their attempts at fixing the worship of them, going more and more awry.

Scorious flashed back to Leo. She gave him a sarcastic clap. "Well done, husband!" She laughed humorlessly, "In a span of a few hours, we've gone from most forgotten to banished."

Scorious snapped her fingers. Abra appeared. "What advice do you have, Abra? Your worshipper's dominate the earth."

"Create new missionaries to change their minds." muttered one voice.

A new voice answered immediately, "That's not the way! We should be the best we can be, without intentionally converting."

A new voice cut through, "If we are going to act on Earth, we should act like their heroes do. For the good of the people living on the planet."

A voice cried out, "The Protector is gaining more and more worship! We must eliminat-"

Abra shook their head, "I am not of one mind. Obviously. We might lose a fight with the Earth heroes. That fight might unleash the unworthy from below. Let us heed The Protector."

"Enough!" Leo cut in. "What foolishness is this? Bowing to humans?" He spat on the floor. "I will not go below."

Scorious smiled, "I thought not." She nodded to Abra, "Thank all of you. It was most enlightening. I will think on what I need to do."

Scorious blinked to Earth. Much had changed. Her clothing was seriously out of date. She was wearing garb from her last visit. She was getting stares. This wouldn't do. She hid herself until she understood the clothing better. Shadows were scarce though. She may have to use something more sophisticated.

"Excuse me ma'am, was there a Ren Faire nearby?" a hooded, brightly colored person asked.

She gasped, "How can you see me?"

The person pointed up, "You're under a street light. You're covered in a misty shadow, which isn't really hiding you. I can also see your body heat. So… Wait, do you not know who I am?"

"No. I don't."

He laughed then. She figured out it was a male voice, very young, maybe. "I'm Bloodwing." He lifted his arms and there was some sort of material that made it look like he had wings. "Pretty awesome to meet you. What rock do you live under?

"Wait, were you one of those people in that other place?" He sniffed and rubbed at his nose. "Fuck, you are." He pushed at something on his wrist. "Let's sit down over there." He gestured towards a bench. "There are some people that want to talk with you."

She let herself get led to the bench. She was lost in thought. How many years had it been since she had been on Earth? 3,000? More? Hmm. Why hadn't she been on Earth? Where had her mind been all that time. Surely court intrigue hadn't been that interesting.

"Hello? are you there?" Bloodwing asked.

She snapped back to focus on the young man. She give him a seriously look. He was not like any human she'd seen last time she was on the planet.

"What year is this?" Scorious asked uncertainly.

"It's 2021." Bloodwing replied, confused.

"Relative to what?"

"Supposedly, it was when Christ was born, but given that the Calendar has been intentionally messed with by both the Romans and the Church, it might be several centuries after the actual event." Bloodwing looked like he was about to continue.

"How long since, the ah, pyramids were built?" Scorious interrupted.

"Hmm, I think the Giza pyramids are like from like 2 or 3000 BCE. So, they're like 5,000 years old or something like that." He held up his hand, "Hold on." He pulled something from his pocket. Tapped at it, swiped his finger around. "Looks like I was pretty darn close. 2500BCE or so. So yea, if you mean Giza, we're 4500 years or so."

"By the Stars, Sun, and Moon. So long. I hardly remember anything." Scorious stared off into nothingness.

She grabbed his arm, "What land are we in? Whose was it during the time of the pyramids?"

Bloodwing harshly pulled his arm free, "We're in the United States. I donno, they spent way more time on Egyptian history than Meso America, alright? I think the Mayans might have been down in South America then." He shrugged.

The wind rustled then. The Protector and a woman lowered to the ground.

Bloodwing sighed in relief, "Thank god. I need to get going." He rubbed the back of his head, "If that's ok, Mother."

Mother nodded in return, "Have a test tomorrow, Wing?"

He nodded.

"Good luck!"

"Thanks, Mother! Protector." He nodded, took two steps, leapt into the air and flew off. Wings beating powerfully.

The Protector took a step forwards, "Why have you come here? I told -"

Scorious waved a hand, "I know what you told Leo. That is immaterial to me. If young Bloodwing is to be believed, the gods of this world were held against our will. I do not remember almost 5,000 years." She glanced about, "5,000 years of amazing growth and change."

Mother placed a placating hand on The Protector's shoulder, "Nevertheless, The Protector's judgment is binding."

"You harshly judge the innocent. Young man." She tilted her head, she gave him a light smile. "I see. Somethings haven't changed?"

The Protector shook his head, "I did not judge you, for punishment. I judged you worthy of executing my judgment on Leo."

"Ma'am," Scorious turned to Mother.

"Please call me Mother." She interjected gently.

"No. I will call no one by that." Scorious grimaced. "Ma'am..." She trailed off. She looked at the stars. "I'm afraid." She turned to the two heroes, tears running down her cheek. "I'm afraid. I haven't been afraid since we cast down our parents. Now something is stirring a fight between you and us. This was by design."

She wiped her face and snapped her fingers.

Mother turned to the Protector, "That woman. She, I was in awe of her. I..." She glanced down. She searched The Protector's face, "What could make someone that powerful, so terrified."

The Protector looked at stars, "Her mother." He cleared his throat. "She doesn't believe Leo is Leo." The Protector sighed, "I might have to make a coffee visit."

"No. I think being visible is the better option. Now, my dear, let's get you out of that ridiculous costume. Are you ever going to be you?"

The Protector shrugged.

Scorious returned to their chambers. Leo emerged from their sauna. He was drying himself off. He barely spared her a glance as he pulled on his robes.

"Where have you been, crone?" He demanded.

"Crone? Is that why you didn't seek to ravage me? I'm simply too old, or have you found another. Someone older perhaps? Or maybe you simply can't any longer."

Leo backhanded her. She caught his slap. She stepped forward and kneed him in his groin. He staggered, but didn't crumple. Not like he used to. His face shifted. His body contorted. He grew. He flexed his arm and pushed her away. Scorious slid back, still holding the arm.

"You are not Leo."

"I'm the best of Leo. I'm what he dreamed of. When you said you were bored. He created me." naLeo said

"What did you do with Leo?"

"Why, he's below, of course!"

Scorious screamed and swung naLeo into the bed beside them. He laughed louder as he crashed through the bed into the floor. Scorious staggered back. "Abra." She whispered to herself. She sprinted out of their bedroom and rushed out of the house.

As she rounded the curve of the mountain they lived upon, naLeo slammed into her. Driving her deep into rock.

"You always saw too much. I should have let you sleep." naLeo gave her a mirthless grin. "Guess this will do."

He began to pummel her. Slamming fist after fist into her. The rock formed a cocoon around her. naLeo must have felt she was secure enough, as he brought down the mountain face to trap her.

She felt strangely calm. Like the rocks were soothing her. Welcoming her into their warm embrace. Her eyes lids were drooping, becoming heavy. She smiled and snuggled into the mountain. It did make a great pillow.

naLeo lounged in his great hall, one of his concubines fed him grapes. A woman, cowled in darkness sat next to him, gently caressing him. "Where did you leave, Scorious?"

"Huh?" naLeo scratched himself. He gulped some wine and belched. "Oh, uh," he gestured vaguely, "In the mountain over there."

She slowly increased the pressure of her caress. She dragged her nail in to his side. A thin trail of blood followed in its wake. "Do you forget who your wife is?"

naLeo snorted, "She's *his* wife. She's nothing to me. I aim higher." He leaned forward and roughly kissed her.

She seemed to tolerate his antics, but did not demonstrate any pleasure herself. Eventually he wore himself out. As he lay panting, she whispered, "If you want to bring me great pleasure. Kill my daughter."

He rolled off her and fell asleep. Scorious's mother growled in frustration.

Abra felt a presence, "Show yourself! This is a stand yer groand state!" A shot gun appeared in his arm.

A projection of Scorious manifested in front of Abra. She gestured to lower the weapon. "May I?" She gestured towards his head.

The god flinched, but allowed her to touch his head. Scorious grimaced immediately. She quickly walked his mindscape. There were thousands of Abras. Some of them sitting together peacefully others locked in mortal combat. She walked and walked. Then realized, she was in a loop. This wasn't just a mindscape.

She fled back out of Abra's mind. She gave him a sad look, "I'm sorry Abra. You're in such pain. I have grave news. Leo isn't Leo. He's changes somehow. Worse still, I believe he's in league with Krotain."

Abra just gave her a sad look, then wondered off. They sat and meditated. As they meditated, the rock seemed to form a cave about him. Their hair grew long and their clothes ragged. She left them there.

She prepared. She only had a few more days until Mother and The Protector returned.

* * *

Meghan was making herself an espresso. She was going through her ritual. It helped calm her. Especially after the past few days, she needed to find her center again. She had just put down her ex, who didn't know she was still alive. That was rough.

A throat was cleared behind her. She turned to find Scorious standing there. As soon as she turned Scorious said, "So, are you the coffee assassin right now, the protector, or someone else?"

"I'm someone else. It's been a hard day. Tomorrow isn't going to be any easier." She loaded her portafilter, put two tiny mugs under, and pushed a button.

"What can I do for you?" Meghan asked.

"Well, we can't stop naLeo and my mother. So, we'll be fighting with you. Given enough time and planning, I could defeat them, but you're coming tomorrow. It's going to be a different fight than you expected. Only bring your strongest, toughest."

Meghan grabbed the mugs. She offered one to Scorious, who replied, "Oh, I'm not physically here. I can't drink it."

Meghan was crestfallen. She sat heavily.

Scorious gave her a sad smile. "I can't drink it, but I can be here with you, drinking it." She put her hand on top of Meghan's and gave her the sensation of touch. They talked.

Eventually Scorious left. Meghan nodded and The Protector stood up. He left to find Mother.

naLeo was impatient. He summoned the heroes again. He summoned their worst enemies. The greatest villains of the time. He leaned back and grabbed some cheese as the humans below figured out what was happening.

He gestured towards Krotian, Scorious's mother, "Summon the gods."

She scowled at him, but complied. Suddenly, the stadium floor was filled with a mix of humans and gods. The gods were furious. They looked right at the box where naLeo and Krotain sat.

naLeo waved a lazy hand, "Fight!" The weakest of mind seemed to lurch into combat between the humans and gods. However, it wasn't the grand spectacle naLeo wanted.

"FIGHT! I COMMAND IT!"

"Ma'am, would you like some coffee." A soft spoken voice asked. She was a short masked woman. She was unassuming.

"Coffee? What's Coffee?" Krotain asked.

"It's a delicious hot beverage. It brings energy and has a complexity of flavor typically reserved for the best wines."

"Sounds delightful." Krotain turned to naLeo, "Why didn't you introduce me to this earlier?"

"I've never had it either," he said absentmindedly.

"I'll bring two then." There was a smile to her eyes. She pulled out a kettle, a strange machine of levers, a grinder, and some small dark beans. She set to work.

As she ground, she gestured towards the brawl below, "Do you have any favorites? Or fights you hope to see?"

naLeo replied, "Yes, the Human's Mother fighting against Scorious. or Mother and The Protector fighting."

"Why the fight, at all, though?" She asked.

Krotain laughed, "To weaken them for conquest. So they can worship their rightful gods. Those humans have gotten too uppity."

"So, this is a blend of South American beans, both Brazilian and Colombian, so you can get an introduction to some different flavors." She said, handing each of them a small glass. "I recommend stirring it, before sipping."

The two stirred, then sipped.

Krotain's eye brows raised, "That was delightful. Though, weak, whatever poison you were using didn't have the KICK you were hoping for." She looked at naLeo and they both laughed.

"I'd never debase coffee with poison. I respect the bean too much. Would you like more?"

She made them several other styles of coffee. As the fight below continued to play out. Distracting them just enough.

"Abra, what are you doing up here?" naLeo shouted suddenly. "You were fighting, someone." He looked about in the skirmish below. "There, you're there!"

"That's the thing with coffee, it really messes with time." the woman said. naLeo turned, but found the Protector instead.

Krotain grinned, "At last." She clapped, "Well done, daughter. You separated us from everyone else."

Scorious stepped out of the floor. She looked at the Protector, "We have an underworld, one where most humans visit when they die. Do you suppose these two would join that underworld?"

Mother joined them. She placed a hand on The Protector's shoulder, "You did well. I'm sorry to have put this burden on you." The Protector patted her hand. Mother continued, "Do you believe they are redeemable?"

The Protector shook his head as he replied,"No. they will continue to dominate. They will try again as soon as we leave. They have tortured Abra for thousands of years. They kidnapped everyone below. They must be destroyed."

Mother looked at Abra, "Do you agree?"

"Turn the other cheek." Spoke a sad voice. "We cannot tolerate tyranny!" cried an angry voice with an American accent. "Eye for an Eye justice!" came an ancient voice.

A stronger voice cut through, "While I am not of one mind. It is clear, that even though turning the other cheek is the ideal, tyranny cannot be allowed to survive in this form. They must be cast down to meet their judgment with the final arbiter."

The Protector nodded. naLeo fell apart, almost as if he was a doll, each limb popping off and then he ceased to be a living thing.

The Protector looked at Scorious, "Killing Krotain would have a universe wide unknowable reaction. I have imprisoned her within this bean. Let us take them to the below."

Scorious lead them to the bottom of the arena. It had been cleared of gods and humans alike. She stood over the center and pulled up. A door appeared.

She opened it. There was an void on the other side. She gestured to Abra to drop naLeo's remains into the void. Mother followed and dropped the coffee bean. The bean was frozen in a moment in time. Scorious shut the door and pushed it below.

Abra screamed and fell to their knees. The moment their knees touched the arena floor, Abra shattered into a thousand smaller versions of Abra. These scattered, running from each other. Factions looked to appear almost immediately.

One of Abra stood, growing quickly, "Thank you. I'm free, free of whatever was trapping me." He looked to Mother and the Protector, "This will have significant impact on Earth." He turned and walked away. He grew lighter as he walked.

Mother watched Abra wander off, then turned to Scorious, "We will take our leave now. We will discuss what happens next between our peoples."

The Protector nodded. As they turned to leave, Scorious grasped the Protector's hand. "I hope to see Meghan again. She's sweet."

Meghan was there, holding Scorious's hand. Scorious smiled and gave Meghan a soft kiss on the cheek. "See you soon."

Suddenly Spiders

"UGH" She huffed. "Alec, turn down *Sleepy Head*" She called to the other room. Every night he played Sleepy Head, like it was some funny joke. She could hear that bassline and that tinny noise and immediately recognize the song. Stupid stupid song.

The song suddenly cut off. Meghan sighed at the sudden silenced. She smiled to herself. She nestled up into her pillow, smelling her own shampoo. So relaxing.

Meghan was dozing when she heard Alec scream. She sat bolt up, her heart hammered in her chest. She rolled out of bed towards the window. It was where she hid the bat. She grabbed that and the knife next to it.

She heard a crash of the window, she glanced out hers and saw Alec hurtling towards the ground. He wasn't screaming.

He wasn't screaming.

Oh god. He wasn't screaming.

A long thin thing gracefully appeared out of Alec's window. It touched on the yellow siding of the house. A second and third followed the first. Eventually eight limbs surrounded Alec's window and a bloated pustule ridden multi-eyed head pulled itself out.

"Fuck you Shelob. You'll not get me." Meghan whispered to herself.

The legs gently prodded for safe purchase on the next step. The yellow paint stained and peeled in the spider's wake. Meghan started, she began to move slowly. Any time a leg moved, she moved. She hoped the spider's own movements would distract it from her.

She made her way across her bed, slowly. Once she was,

generally, out of the immediate view of the spider, she moved a bit more quickly. She opened the door. Something held it shut. Meghan was able to pull it open about a foot, but then a resistance would build and the door would spring back closed. She pulled the door open a sliver and peeked out. There was massive spider silk spread across the hallway. As if the hideous thing had made a web.

Her throat caught, "Alec. That fucking song." She stifled a sob.

She swung open her butterfly knife and pulled open the door. She cut strands of web, just until the door opened farther. She didn't want the spider to have an easy time getting out. Meghan, though, took after her favorite artist, Meghan Thee Stallion, so she really had to squeeze to make it through the door.

Once she managed to squeeze through, the door sprang back into her face. It hit her nose hard enough to make her need to sneeze. "FUCK" Meghan gasped and let out her breath. She gently closed the door, while scrunching her nose, trying desperately to avoid a sneeze. She heard glass crack on the other side of the door. The window would give out soon.

With that she turned towards the hallway. Her room was farthest from the stairs, the bathroom she'd shared with Alec was ground zero for web strands. It looked webs had shot out of it all at once. The door was shattered, the top corner was rocking, bouncing, hinges half torn off, against a strand caught on the ceiling.

The web hadn't been too sticky against her knife, so she gently pushed against the strand from the bathroom. Her hand immediately fastened to the webbing.

She sneezed.

She heard a thunder of legs. Things fell from the wall. Glass shattered. A mass slammed against the wall.

Meghan quickly cut the strand holding her hand. She elected against cutting the strand entirely, just a piece of it. Enough to get her hand free. She looked at the mess in front of her. There was no way she could get through there. It looked like that time Alec had hit a Silly String can with a sledge hammer to see what would happen.

She glanced behind her. The end of the hall window. It was surrounded by Christmas lights. She ran to the window and quickly pulled it up. She popped the screen out and pulled it into the house. She tried to be as quiet as possible. She moved back towards her room, sneezed again. It was a terrible fake sneeze, but it triggered more bashing in her bedroom.

She shuffled back to the window. She stuffed her bat into the back of her shirt and her knife in her pjays, praying it would stay in place. She stuck her head out the window and grabbed the lights and jumped out.

She hung in the air for a moment. Then the staples began to pop from the window frame. Each pop dropped Meghan lower. She couldn't help but yelp. As the staples gave out she accelerated towards the ground. She spun out of control. She swung this way and that. Through the chaos of her descent, she saw a leg daintily reach around the corner.

Then a second one. She heard a crashed from her bedroom as the massive spider lurched out her window.

She felt herself swing towards the legs. She glanced up at the roof. The staples were pulling towards the front of the house. Toward her bedroom. Toward the monster.

Meghan's hands slipped on the lights. The jerk of the dropping and her weight conspired against her. The lights cut into her hand, tearing her skin raw. Meghan realized she wasn't too far above the bushes, she picked a bush as a target and let go.

Her momentum carried her into the wrong bush. It was all she could do to get her arms up to protect her eyes as she flew into a trestle of rose bushes. Her arms were gashed as she slammed into the calla lily next to the roses. She'd missed the big soft looking bush.

Meghan staggered out of the landscaped shrubbery and onto the lawn proper. She looked about wildly. Trying to find the spider. Meghan stepped back and staggered on something. As she whirled, she pulled out her bat. It was Alec.

He groaned.

She knelt down, sobbing, "You're alive?"

He moaned. His moan turned into a shriek.

Meghan turned and saw the massive spider. She was able to make out the head in more detail. It was her mom's.

"Oh god, Alec, what did you do? What happened." Meghan whispered.

His only response was a weak grunt.

"Mom, I know we need to work through some stuff, but this is ridiculous!" Meghan called. Her heart thumped and her breath was fast. She swallowed.

In response, her mother, Darcy, face split. Darcy spat black bile towards Meghan and Alec. It missed wide to the right, hitting the walk up to their house behind Meghan.

"Now Darcy, knock that off." Meghan forced her words out.

The spider charged forward. Meghan readied her bat. She swung hard.

The impact was hand numbing. Her bloody fingers dropped the bat. Darcy kicked her. Meghan was thrown backwards. She landed hard, her knife flew from her pocket. It slid next to Alec.

Meghan rolled and pushed herself up, she scanned for her bat. Right behind Darcy.

"Are you dancing to that stupid song, again?" Darcy screeched.

"What song is that? WAP?" Meghan cried, laughing. "Get a Bucket and a mop."

Darcy charged again. Meghan lunged under Darcy, avoiding the spider's legs. She slid toward the bat.

Darcy slid to a stop, rotated, and charged. She was fast, but Meghan was faster. She got to her bat and held it between her legs. In an attempt to crush Meghan, Darcy dropped. Instead she impaled herself on Meghan's bat. The bat tore between two carapace sections. Releasing spider bile and blood.

The liquid immediately began to eat away at Meghan. Darcy screeched and slouched away from, pulling the bat from Meghan's slick hands. Meghan got to her feet and staggered towards the hose. She turned it on full blast, hoping to get the retched liquid off of her.

Meghan was lost in her pain. Unable to think or see straight. She'd managed to clean herself off, when she was suddenly flying through the air. She slammed into the garage door.

Darcy staggered. The bat still lodged into her. There were guts pouring out of the wound. One of hind legs and another of her mid legs vainly attempted to grab the bat and remove it. Every time they got a hold of it, they'd hit something as they pulled it out.

Meghan stood, dazed. She saw a flash in the air. Something hit the driveway and slid to her. Her knife bounced off her foot. She looked for

Alec, he was hiding somewhere.

Darcy moved closer, angled to keep her wounded stomach away from her daughter. She pulled part of herself up onto the house.

Meghan knelt, getting the knife ready for her strike.

Darcy suddenly lurched up at Meghan. The bat slid out from Darcy's gut, clattering to the ground. The spider staggered at the sudden release.

WAP started playing behind Darcy on a set of tinny phone speakers. Meghan struck. She jumped onto the garage door and used an indentation to launch herself up into Darcy. Meghan stabbed into the center of Darcy's forehead.

Darcy reared back, pulling away from Meghan. She staggered toward the source of the song. She screeched fell backwards into the house. Ichor poured from the rupture in her stomach. She screamed one last time, before she stilled.

Alec limped over to Meghan. They helped each other walk away from the garage door. Alec glanced at Meghan, "Did you really use an indentation from your butt to stab mom in the face?"

Meghan laughed. Then began to wheeze.

Emergency response vehicles pulled up to the house.

He sat his in favorite chair. His breath was ragged in his throat. He leaned his head back, breathing deep, trying to catch a breath he'd never catch. His breath rattled in his throat as the light in his eyes dimmed.

"Damn," I muttered. "FUCK!" I yelled. I looked over at Danny, "Did you really have to hit him like that? I mean, for fuck's sake, look at him!" I forcefully gesture at the formerly living man in the well worn chair.

Danny looked down, like a puppy. His eyes all big and sorry. He even had the gall to scuff his shoe against the ground like some innocent lost kid. "I'm sorry boss."

I skewered him with a look, "Danny, did you *really* just say sowwy to me? What are you a scene kid or something?"

Danny had the awareness to look ashamed, actually ashamed and not pretend ashamed. "Yea, I won't do it again boss."

I rubbed my face, "Danny, you're 45 years old. You're older than me, fucking act like it." I turned and looked at the mess Danny made.

I rubbed my eyes, getting an eyelash in my eye, which caused me to gawp about for a minute.

"You ok, boss?"

I sighed a long ragged sigh, "Yea. I'm fine. Ok, well, get your bag and grab him and the chair. We gotta take both." I pause, "Just don't touch or take anything else."

I leave Danny to get his bag set up. I call over my shoulder, "Leave it open until I finish searching the place."

I don't know if he heard me or not. With my luck, Danny probably trapped himself in his own bag. I scoffed at the idea. I quickly searched the place. More accurately, I used my wand to search the place. It's a great little tool. It finds hidden compartments and magic auras identifying specific items you're looking for.

The outline of the dead man's safe appeared. It's one of those where only the door is visible. Real fuckery those. I quickly cast a trap detection spell. I blew out a breath. "Fuuuuuck. Magic and mundane."

Danny shambled into the room. He flicked his hair out of the way. It's style cut in a style that was popular when he was in his 20s, well it was popular for people that were my age when he was in his 20s. He definitely was one of those guys that went after girls still wearing their ribbons.

I looked at the first trap. It's mundane, but significant. I expand the details of the trap with my binocoles. I cast a cantrip to allow me to manipulate small objects. After a few moments of inspection, I figured out how to disarm the trap.

I worked forward, trap after trap. Until I hit the first magical trap. I stood up, stretched and cracked my back. I glanced around, my eyes large trying to focus on the room.

"I'm hungry boss." Danny whined.

"Then eat."

He rubbed the back of his neck, "I, uh, I" he poked his index fingers together, "I forgot to bring food."

"Are you a fucking child? Then eat the dead man's food! I need to concentrate."

I squatted back down and began to work on the magical traps. These are good. Very good traps. The trap maker looked like he had been a blacksmith in the past. Each trap was interlocked with the next and the last. However, like a blacksmith's puzzle, once you find the thread, they fell apart quickly.

An hour later, I stood, the whole puzzle was a snake eating it's tail. There was no way to break it without a key. But there was always a way to get into a lock. These traps were just locks. That's all they are, just another lock. I began to pace. I ran directly into Danny. I staggered back and nearly fell into the traps. I was on my back staring up at the ceiling. I saw the answer on the ceiling.

It was like one of those sculptures, where if you look at it from one direction, it's a person's face, or a scene from an epic battle, but if you look at it from another direction, it's a heap of trash. I didn't need to destroy the trap moving from front to back or back to front. I could attack it from another angle.

While I laid on my back, I shut my eyes and dove into the magical energy. I attacked it from inside the magic. As if I was a part of the trap, I was just more magic. I saw it then. the thread was back inside on itself. Neatly done, but not quite well enough for someone with my skill.

The whole set of traps collapsed and the door to the safe triggered. Forcing out another safe. One that would fit in our bag.

I stood up and looked at Danny, "Well, grab the safe and drop it on the chair in the bag. Then we can get out of here and get some real food."

He grabbed his hat off his head, where did he get that hat? "I'm sooo sowwy, I sh -"

"GODS FUCKING DAMN IT!" I glared up at the man. I pulled out my bag and carefully opened it. I knew this might happen, so I had spares. They are just expensive to use.

"Danny put the safe in the bag." I ordered.

He gave me a hang dog look, "Yes, sir." I looked up at the ceiling in exasperation. My wand suddenly triggered, there was another trap there. Some how that sly dog had hidden the trap within the safe.

"Danny, STOP! put the safe down on that chair there." He glumly put the safe on a stool.

"Did I do something wrong? Are you mad at me?"

"What? No. I think it's another trap." I snapped back.

I took the bag and slowly moved it up and over the safe. It's hard to describe the feeling of putting a portal bag in another portal bag. The best way I've heard it described is reality is shrieking.

I immediately threw up, dropped to the ground, and shit myself.

Danny did the same.

Fortunately, between the two of us falling, the bag fell away from the "safe" and we regained our senses.

I staggered to my feet and grabbed my extra set of clothes from my bag. I tossed Danny another set too. After we'd changed, I pulled out the Tonic. It was the only way to truly recover from one of those events. It's expensive, but the price of the work that we do.

I cast a quick cantrip to make the safe lighter. We packed up our bags. Danny took the safe, and we used a portal to get the fuck out of there.

We stepped out into my shop. Dawn was already peaking through the window. It'd been a long night, but it was annoying that she'd showed up already. The second sun hadn't even risen yet!

She started pounding on the door. I glanced over at Danny, the son of a bitch was hiding. I sighed and opened the door.

"Good morn, Dawn. As you can see, we only just got back. We desperately need to clean up." I said wearily.

"The burning sky, you do! You have my stuff or not?" She demanded.

"You didn't tell us there were two safes. Nor did you tell us one was a portal."

She took a step back and sniffed at me "Hmm, maybe you ought to make a trip to the salty sea and clean up."

I chuckled, "You think the sunken lord would have us?" I waved away the question before she could answer. "I have a shower here." I heard the water start, "Which Danny has apparently decided to use."

Dawn laughed.

I gave her a sharp look. She laughed harder. "We will come to your temple when we are finished here."

"Unthinkable! You rabble entering the Temple of the Flaming Twins? Unthinkable. You are their antithesis." She put her hand to her chest.

"Fine. Fine, fine!" I mutter with exhaustion. I pulled the portal safe over to a work station. I began to analyze the lock. I pulled on my biconoles. The lock mechanism was relatively novel. Certainly wasn't something that most people would have access too. I pulled my wand out and manipulated it, so it turned into a pick set.

The wand highlighted wards within the lock.

I leaned back and glared at Dawn, "You, or someone, put the Flaming Twins and the Fallen Brother in this lock as part of the mechanism?"

She looked away, sheepishly. She turned back, "Well, yes, the Flaming TWINS! Are the best sort of security we could think of."

"The Fallen Brother?" I asked impatiently.

"There are heretical documents in here that we cannot have getting out!"

I looked at her through my binocoles. Then I flicked my wand to activate the shop security. The parameter flared up in my binocoles.

I leaned back my chair, "Ah. I see."

"You're blinded by the Fallen Brother. You cannot see." Dawn cried.

I twitched my wand again. Security wards triggered. Screams. The shop was surrounded by screams. Dawn struck then, I rolled off the back of my stool. She staggered back as my feet swept up towards her.

She grabbed her charm and summoned two globes of fire. They began to orbit her. She shot her hand out, the smaller of the two, the one representing the sun in the sky, flew towards me.

I dove behind our counter, back towards the shop shower and kitchen. The small sun swung unnaturally towards me, skimming the ground, leaving streaks of fire in its wake. I lashed out with my wand, I struck the ball and sent it back towards Dawn.

She deftly pulled the sun back into orbit around her, sending the other flaming twin at me.

It was then Danny burst out of the shower. He was still naked, but he wasn't a sad shameful man any longer. He caught the ball, as if it was nothing and burst it in his hands. He lunged and grabbed Dawn, even as she swung the other sun onto his head. She cried out as Danny burst her head.

The flame collapsed, leaving nothing by a few burnt marks on Danny's cheek. He bellowed in rage and rushed out of the shop.

The other Golden Sun Templars were still working their way out of my traps. They never stood a chance against Danny.

In the time it would take me to walk around our shop, he'd killed a dozen men, bringing what remained of their corpses to the shop door. He left them there, like a cat. He staggered through the door. He looked at me, breathing heavy. Burn marks across his body rapidly healing, blood dripping down his body.

He wiped the rage from his face. He seemed to deflate. He shrunk back into that sad man.

I sighed, mourning the loss of who Danny should be, yet again.

"Why don't you go wash up. I'll take care of your offerings. I think you've made the Banished Brother happy today." I smiled at him. "As for me, brother, you've made me proud."

To hunt and be hunted

"HOOaaaak" The cry rips from this one's throat. It is a honk of terror and pain. This one pulls. "OOaaaoooOOOOOo" this one screeches.

Tears well in this one's eyes. The herd, bounds away, leaving this one alone.

"AAAAAooooOOOooo" Alone. This one never wanted to be alone. The herd is life. The herd is safety.

Cold teeth bite into this one's back heartside leg. Life blood flows from the bite. This one looks down. The jaws are far into this one's leg. The bone is popping and grinding. It's too much. This one lays down. Crying out. Begging to no longer be this one, but one of many again. This one hears the strange steps of the two legged. It's their detached jaw. It's evil.

"AooooOOOOOOOOOOOOooooooo" this one cries.

A small two legged monster gets closer to this one. It smells of the many, the herd, but it is not of the herd. Strange one.

The two legged strange one mimics sounds of mother. Mother is no longer part of the many. Mother was taken by the firey teeth of the wolf.

This one learned much from other. This one tried to stay with the many. Now the strange one pulled on this one's power. The strange one pulled and pushed. Trying to dominate. It is not mating season. Why is the strange one trying to dominate. The two legged ones are grunting and groaning.

"AAOoooOoooOOOOooooOOO" This one shrieks. An tine of power stabbed into this one's chest.

This one's world goes dark for a moment. Suddenly this one can see the body of this one. It is being lifted above and away from the body. This one is even more alone. This one cannot cry out any longer. The two legged are crying louder and louder. Crying for this one.

This one feels the blunt teeth of the strange one. Feels the swallow of the strange one. This one finds itself looking out at this one's body. This one feels a caress. A gentle touch. This one's vision blurs. The strange one can see and feel this one. The chanting rises into a lovely call of the wild.

I shudder. It's always disorientating joining with an animal like that. I can still smell me, strange one. I can taste the fear.

I cast about in my mind, the scrub deer joined the herd of my soul fairly easily. It was so lonely. So afraid. The beaver helped make it feel welcome. It had met and known a number of beavers. So it was a bit of a come homing. The hawk joined the deer, resting on it's antlers.

"Now, Thijsen, run, join with the Deer!" cried my teacher.

I bound off. I began to run and call to the deer. "This one" as it like to call itself. I asked for it help, I asked "This one, could you help me flee from a wolf?"

"This one is fleet of hoof and has learned many ways to out run and out smart the wolf."

I let out a deerlike hoot and found myself floating over the forest floor. I barely ruffled the leaves on trees. The rotting leaves under hoof didn't crinkle. Not a footprint was left behind.

I ran to a lake's edge and bounded in. I found the beaver, I call him Blunt, and dove deep into the lake. I popped up and swam to the opposite shoreline. I found the hawk and flew across again, there I swooped down and returned to "This One". I returned back to my teacher and nuzzled her.

She punched my nose and I turned back into my self. She laughed at me. After catching herself, she spoke, "We must honor your deer. He gave everything he had to become a part of you. No, *you* must honor him and leave nothing to rot."

I nodded and began to carve my former body up. This was always the most disorienting part of the joining. It was intentional. To separate man and beast. To create separate personalities, without shattering the joining. I shuddered as I plunged the knife into my abdomen. I quickly gutted the body. Removing the intestines. I worked swiftly to avoid poisoning the flesh. This deer, though it was a scrub deer, was still large enough to feed the tribe tonight, provide clothing for at least one, and material for weapons for multiple warriors.

I eventually finished butchering the deer. I took both antlers to fashion weapons with them. This was how our tribe was known. The Deer Tribe. Several of us shared the weight of carrying the butchered meat back to our village. It was a small village but we had what we needed.

As was expected of a recently joined man, I built the bonfire. I smoked the ribs. Stoked the stew. Make the broth. Sausages were made by the elderly, those too feeble to carry meat any longer.

The fire burnt bright that night. The deer constellation was high, it was dominant. As if the very universe was celebrating me. I fell asleep with a warm belly beside the fire that night. My weapons had been crafted. I was ready for the world. I was a man.

Screams woke me. The village square was filled with smoke or fog or both. It was hard to tell. The fires had burned low and were smoldering. Another cry pierced the night. One of our huts burst into flames.

A shadow darted past me. A doe. A bird that had no reason to be flying at night cried out, it dove another direction.

I ran. As I ran, I dove into This One for speed. We ran, fast and far.

Howls of wolves followed behind us. I ran using everything I learned from This One to leave no trail. To leave no scent, no sound. The wolves still came. I swung towards the forest. I bound close to the traps. The traps we had reset after catching This One.

A wolf howled in pain. The pack scattered. They recognized steel man teeth as easily as This One did. I began to sing. I sang the tuning song. One from the Deer tribe had never joined with a wolf. None had ever dared.

The wolf heard me coming. It bared its teeth and snapped at me. I pushed up it's jaw with my antlers. I quickly stabbed the heart, cutting it out, as I sang.

I could feel the living soul. The soul of the wolf as I sang and I bit down.

I felt the other soul crash into my own. It wasn't just A soul though, it was a cacophony of souls. It was like me. Though it was a pack rather than herd. There was a man in that pack. He screamed and raged. He charged me. I gored him with my antlers. He never stood a chance. He turned to mist around my antlers. Dissolving, scattering like a swarm of bats. I swung my antlers about impotently.

I could hear myself singing. Trying to keep the joining going. I felt this invader trying to destroy me. Trying to own me from the inside.

I focused. I became the man. I ran, cried out. I, Martin ran back to the village. Then something Forced me to turn back to the woods. Why would I go to the woods? My village was celebrating a great successful raid over the weak Deer tribe.

No, no! Not the woods. I didn't have a choice. My legs acted of my own accord. I saw a body in a trap. I knelt down. It looked like me.

I was suddenly pushed aside.

I am Thijsen! I pulled my antler knife out and began to butcher the body. I quickly make a small fire and cooked and ate small strips of meat.

I heard a commotion behind me. I quickly turned into This One and fled. I smiled, I became Martin and walked back towards the traps.

"Friends, I need your help!" I cried out. Why am I saying that? I should run towards them. I looked at my hands, what meat am I chewing. That skin, that marking.

I retch. What animal have I become a part of. No, not an animal. Monster.

I become a hawk, flying up into the trees next to the traps. I watch silently as a wolf cautiously pads towards where Martin's body lay trapped. I smile to myself. The wolf's fore paw triggered the trap. I jump down, song on my lips, antlers gouging into the chest. I quickly rip out and devour the man's heart.

I hunt every man down that attacked my village. I eat their heart. They become part of Us. part of the collective of we. The many. This One is happy to be part of the many. The herd and the pack is strong.

We find ourselves resting by a stream, when a familiar scent happens by. It smells of the pack member Thijsen's teacher. We become him. It is a challenge to contain the multitudes in him. He's small and was weak. I'm surprised I was able to survive eating Martin's heart, let alone the dozen other men that attacked our village.

I walk gingerly into Teacher's camp. She knows I'm coming. I smell distrust on her, though. I bow as I approach the fire, "Teacher, I didn't know anyone else had survived the ambush! I'm happy to see you." I lurch forward, hoping for a hug. I miss her so much. I feel a heat rise up in me. I see her as a woman not just a teacher. She is a hard beautiful woman.

I push back against the WE. I need to stay in control if I have any hope of rejoining a village. Of growing my herd, my pack. I glance at the fire and lick my lips, as my eyes dart back to her.

"It seems you've grown up since we last talked. Not just a man. But a lusting man. Hunting more than just food." She sounded sad.

I tilted my head at her, "What do you mean? I've just missed you, is all."

"I've missed Thijsen too. It's a shame, isn't it?"

"We love Thijsen. There's no shame here. We aren't ashamed, why would we be shamed?" We said. "We are Thijsen. I am Thijsen. I am This One. I am a Beaver named Blunt. I am a beautiful hawk named Lady."

"You're more than just those, aren't you?" She asked.

"Martin's here too." Thijsen responds before We can stop him. Thijsen is thrust back. We act. She will be ours.

Her antler lashed out at our stomach. Before we could touch her legs, her talons were raking our face. Her beak snipped at the back of our neck. We spun, she was already falling, a beaver biting our groin.

We staggered back. WE became a wolf. We tripped over our entrails. We turned into a bird. She dove onto our backs. Driving us to the ground.

We turned into a bear. She became human and drove her antlers into our throat. Our head was trapped in the earth. We tried to swat and paw her away.

She began to chant. Thijsen wailed. We tried to shut him up. A knife dug deep into our chest. We saw ourselves. We were in our heart. We'd all seen this before. We waited for the dull bite of human teeth.

She rotated our heart. She gave us a sad look as she continued chanting and casually tossed us into the fire.

We heard the sizzle and saw the world burn away. We howled.

An Unfortunate Man

Antoine gripped his console. His knuckles grew white. His arms shook with the effort. He glanced about and laughed nervously. He relaxed a little as he saw the man next to him doing the same thing.

"You know Sam," Antoine tried to say as casually as possible. His voice quavered despite his best efforts (his efforts were never what most people would call "best"). "I am always surprised by the power of an exploding planet." He laughed and waved his hand. "I don't know why? It's a planet, you know?" He laughed. It was an unconvincing laugh.

"Don't talk to me Antoine. People around you..." Sam hesitated. Sam made the right decision and turned back to his work. Antoine really should be ignored.

Antoine sighed. He was dejected, but expected the rebuff. "Yea, I'm that guy who left his partner on a planet scheduled for destruction."

"Shut the fuck up Antoine." Sam said through gritted teeth. He was seething. "That partner, that partner was my life partner!" Sam stood, thrusting back his chair. "You dumb son of a bitch!"

It was the wrong time for Sam to thrust his chair back. Unfortunately for Sam, the thrust caused it to run directly into the mad space wizard that powered the machine destroying planets. Antoine helpfully pointed over Sam's shoulder.

Sam leans in close to Antoine, "This better not be a fucking joke." He turns around. The mad space wizard while easily angered knows how to play the moment.

Sam spins, expecting another low ranking officer or something like that. He ended up staring right into the chest of the mad space wizard. She hated when men stare at her chest. This didn't help Sam's cause.

Sam quickly staggered back, hoping to recover something by looking like he was a clumsy mess. The mad space wizard, though, she knew the only clumsy mess on the ship, at least clumsy enough to behave like Sam was acting, was Antoine.

"I'm sorry your madness." Sam muttered.

She laughed, "Not my normal title. At least you're honest about your opinion."

She waved her hand and turned Sam into a puppy. She picked him up and petted him. "If you shit on my robes, I'll kill you and feed you to Antoine. NO!" She grabbed Sam by the scruff of his neck, "I'll make Antoine watch you." She laughed.

Antoine wept. He already had three dogs, five cats, and a bird. The bird was the most challenging, it was a large owl and often ate other animals. Sam was small enough that Antoine would likely wake up to the Owl, Oliver, eating Sam atop Antoine's head in the middle of the night.

Antoine tried to hide in his work. Which, given the state of AI and his complete ineptitude in everything, was more or less playing and losing at solitaire.

"Antoine!" came the cry. He shuddered. He knew what it meant. "It is time for you to service me."

The mad space wizard had many partners. She often would move from ship to ship and find someone that interested her. That person would move up through the ranks. Not because the mad space wizard force people to promote them, but because the mad space wizard would bless them with great luck and success.

With Antoine, she had cursed him. She jealously held onto him. So, Antoine was not allowed any close friends except for animals. He was hers. That curse destroyed the lives of everyone around him. He used to be a graceful musician. He was considered one of the best. Now, his voice cracked and was always just slightly out of tune.

He was accused of leaving his partner on the doomed planet. Everyone knew it wasn't true. The mad space wizard wouldn't let the partner back on the shuttle. No one could blame the mad space wizard though. They destroyed planets.

Antoine stood glumly. He was actually winning solitaire for once.

He pushed in his chair and put a sign on it. Antoine's chair. The owl was a commander that had sat in Antoine's seat and refused to move when Antoine came back from the toilet.

Antoine didn't blame the owl for eating on his head. It's kind of a fair thing to do. He glanced down at Sam. He had to write up the report and notify the next of kin. Antoine sighed gently to himself. He'd have to tell the next of kin that Sam was a puppy and likely would get eaten by a the giant Cmd Oliver Owl.

"I'm on my way grand space mistress!" Antoine called cheerily. The nearest officer cringed. Somehow looking both terrified and relieved Antoine was leaving the bridge.

Antoine knew most people thought this was some weird sex thing between them. Mad space wizard never did that with Antoine. He believes that was her original intent. She often would use and abuse her artists and musicians (and they, of course, would have amazing careers). The opposite was true for Antoine. His careers were dismal. He was stuck as a low ranking Imperial officer and no one would hire him for his singing or sculpting.

He arrived at her quarters. He knew he'd be there singing, playing, and sculpting all night. Mad space wizard had a thing where she liked to fill the doomed planets with beautiful things. Everything Antoine sang, played (on various instruments), and sculpted ended up on the planet before it was destroyed. Often it was the only art ever on the planet. In other cases it became the best art the planet ever saw.

When he left his partner on the planet. Mad space wizard made them stay, because they had intentionally listened to the music and saw the sculptures. Many of them were of the mad space wizard. Others were people aboard the ship or paintings of amazing landscapes.

That partner would have broken Antoine's curse. breaking of that curse would have broken mad space wizard's power, or so Antoine believed. That couldn't happen!

"What would you like today?" Antoine asked. He was calm. There wasn't much else she could do to him and death would be an escape at this point.

She walked up and caressed his cheek. "Do you hate me, Antoine?"

"No, of course not. I love you my mistress." Antoine lied.

"It hurts me when you lie." She grabbed his tie, as all officers in the Empire must wear times while on duty, and pulled him up into his tip toes into a kiss. She was a towering dominating presence.

Antoine staggered back. This was new. New, with the mad space wizard was scary. She tasted of blueberries and a hint of sadness. She sat, looking small and alone. She offhandedly gestured. Antoine knew this was an order to ignore normal pretenses. So, he pulled off his tie and loosened his shirt before sitting next to her.

"What's wrong my lady?" He asked.

"Destroying planets has lost it's charm. Concentrating your art made it fun for a while. I knew that I was destroying the most beautiful thing on that world and in the Empire. That was fun, it brought me a lot of joy and made the destruction easier." She wiped a tear from her cheek.

She gave Antoine a look, "But it's come at a huge cost. Your life is miserable. Your grace is gone, unless I'm directing it. I do this more often," she gestured to Sam. The puppy was sleeping in a kennel nearby.

Antoine shrugged, "You have the power to do these things, though. So you do them."

She laughed, she'd never had a sad laugh before. That was new, "Yes, and it earns me the name 'mad space wizard.'" She wiped an eye, "That's not very nice you know. The blessings and yours is a blessing, come with a cost. Most of the time I bear the cost. It's a slight loss of me. In your case it was a loss for both of us. You lost your grace. I was forced to destroy anyone that saw your grace. every planet I destroyed, had to be destroyed. The grandeur of your grace demanded its destruction."

"Please end this." Antoine replied. "Just let me be an excellent artist again. I don't want to be the best ever, any longer."

"I can't help it, that's what your need demanded." She sighed. "I will remove your blessing after you make one more sculpture. Carve me, but make me kind."

She led him to the studio. There was a beautiful piece of stone. He touched it. He'd never felt anything like it before. It breathed and responded to his touch. He smelled blueberries.

"This is from the planet you just destroyed." He said, not asking anything nor knowing what he was saying.

She nodded. Touching the stone. "I'll feed your pets."

Antoine didn't even notice her departure. He was fevered. He could see her in the stone. It was like she had been imprisoned by the stone. That this was the real space mistress. That the mad space wizard wasn't the real her. That what he was seeing here was the truth.

He quickly started his work. While he was making quick sure movement, they were small but precise. He was gentle and loving. He carved for three days. He paused long enough only to use the bathroom and eat when she made him eat.

His space mistress stood naked when he was getting close and putting in the finishing touches. He finally put down his tools. He stepped back and blinked in confusion. A new color had seemed to seep into the stone.

He glanced at the woman and the sculpture, they were identical. The space wizard walked to look at herself. They were exact mirrors. No, that's not true. The sculpture, looked like it was carrying less. Like it was a lighter being.

Antoine blinked. He swore the sculpture's chest was moving. That it was breathing. Then the space wizard leaned forward and kissed the sculpture.

She waved Antoine to leave. He grudgingly did.

Several hours later, Antoine was awoken from a deep sleep. It had been filled with strange dreams. He hadn't dreamed in years. Not since she had given him what he thought he needed. He found her at his door.

"Antoine," She said. "Thank you for freeing me. My name is Epiphany. Your mad space wizard is letting us go. She said you'll find your account filled with more money than you'll ever know what to do with."

Antoine took Epiphany, hooded, to the crew's Rest and Relaxation shuttle. A place where everyone would see the two of them. They'd never left the ship together, but it still worried Antoine. Worried Antoine what people would say having the mad space wizard on their Shuttle. They wouldn't know it's not her.

As they were sitting on the shuttle eating breakfast a song came on over the restaurant speakers. Antoine began to hum.

A crew member turned, "Huh, I had no idea you could sing."

Antoine smiled.

Chaos at the Climate Convention

He took a deep breath and gave them the finger. Then he ran. Despite his bluster, he wasn't a one man army. He was one man and he was intentionally pissing off the cops. It's not like it was difficult to piss off cops. You look at them funny, fart near them, or do something as silly as giving them the finger and they'll be all up in arms, often literally, about it.

Steven was a distraction. His friends were going to do a sit in at the climate talks. They were mostly doing it for kicks. The sit ins would amount to more action than the politicians inside..

Steven was the fastest and had the most endurance, being a marathon runner. He'd intentionally started far enough away that he could get up to speed if one of the cops was a good sprinter. He dropped jacket to show off the back of his shirt. It had a giant X through the thin blue line punisher logo. He may have added some "blood" spraying out the side of the logo too, just for laughs.

That did it. He heard the cops thundering behind him. Some of them were yelling at him. He looked over his shoulder, there was a line backer looking dude that was sprinting for all he was worth. Steven sprinted. The man was easily keeping pace. Steven began to duck and weave through the crowd heading towards the conference.

The man slowed down. Steven continued jogging away. He was suddenly barreled into. He was knocked to his back, a dogs muzzle suddenly in his face.

Steven laid still, very still. He breathed slowly. Calmly. He tried to exude calm. The K9's handler was anything but calm. Steven could feel his rage and agitation from where he was laying. The dog was clearly torn between the two energy types, but the handler was winning out.

"What are you doing?" a voice cried out. "He was just running and you set at dog on him? Boo!"

"Let him go!" another person called. It turned into a chant, "Let him go. Let him go."

The handler pulled the dog back. It was getting agitated by the crowd.

Steven stayed laying on the ground. The dog was easily within range. He didn't want to risk being bitten.

The crowd began to press in around Steven. The dog started to bark and strain at the leash. The cop was looking disparate.

The leash slipped.

The dog, jaws slavering, lunged at the nearest protester. The dog went high and bit.

Blood spurted. The protester dropped.

The dog shook. Hard. It pulled back and dropped what was in its mouth. Steven looked at the protester in horror as the man was clutching at a ruined throat. Pink foam collected around the trachea.

The cop gaped at the dying man. His radio rasped repeatedly.

Suddenly, the line backer cop was there. He tackled the dog, who was foaming at the mouth. His hand was bit, blood oozed out. He punched the dog in the throat. He let go backed up and coughed.

The dog glanced about looking for a way out. It turned and launched itself passed its handler. He was able to grab a hold of the leash and hold on tight. The dog took exception to that. It turned and lunged towards the man's face. His face turned to red as the dog turned and ran off.

Steven, feeling somewhat responsible, sprinted after the dog. He grabbed at the leash, barely missing.

The linebacker was next to him. He called, "Distract the dog. I'll tackle him and then we can muzzle him."

"Sure thing." Steven replied. He turned on the jets and sprint up next to the dog. The dog turned a baleful gaze towards Steven. He lunged at him.

Steven twisted and darted away from the beast. He felt his shirt pull. The fabric tore as the dog jerked his head back away from Steven.

Steven checked to see where the dog was pivoting, to see the linebacker had grabbed the dog again.

Linebacker was far enough back the dog was having issues getting his jaws on the man. Steven ran a loop around the dog. Menacing the dog as much as he dared. Linebacker was able to get a better grip on the animal. He had managed to get a hold of the collar and pulled up tight. The animal was frantic. It pivoted this way and that, trying to get a tooth on Linebacker.

"Come here, kid." Linebacker called.

Steven finished his loop and got behind the dog. "What's next?"

Linebacker grunted, "You grab the collar with both hands. This dog is STRONG."

Steven followed the directions. Once Steven had a grasp on the collar Linebacker put his hand on the dogs head and started to push down towards the snout. Once below the eye, he pushed down firmer, pushing the dog's head towards it's chest.

Steven lowered the dog to the ground. Linebacker, suddenly moved with his other hand. He pulled out his gun and shot the dog in the chest.

The dog whined, wheezed, then died.

Steven staggered away from the dog. He fell limbless to the ground.

"You dumb mother fucker. This is your fault." Linebacker screamed.

He rushed Steven and jumped on him. He pounded Steven's head off the sidewalk. "Stan was a friend of mine. Zeus was a good dog!"

A rush of blue flew over Steven. He heard raised voices, but was too dazed to make out the words.

A short time later, Steven found himself in the hospital. He was handcuffed to the bed and a cop was standing outside his room. He was still half dazed from his beating.

A nurse swooped into the room. "Good you're awake." She paused and glanced at the cop, "You've been, allegedly, involved in an incident, well two. Someone bombed the climate event which may have been possible because the police chased you. The second is the police dog attack. We've run some tests and the dog had a virus. We're not sure what it is, but you're under quarantine until we understand it."

Steven grunted, "Can I have some water?"

The nurse checked the IV, "Hmm. I'll get a small cup."

She started to head out, but she turned back. She glanced at the cop, "You know not to talk to the cops without your lawyer, right?" She hurried past the cop.

"Hey!" The cop yelled, Steven saw him try to grab the nurse. She dodged him, in that way women know how to dodge handsy men.

Steven felt terrible. His eyes were bulging. His fingers were pruning. Now his feet were cold.

The handcuff burned. He screamed in pain. He pulled at the handcuff. Suddenly, the pain disappeared. Steven relaxed and sunk into the bed. Blood dripped onto the floor from the cut the handcuff's left.

Steven awoke to tornado warning alarms ringing. Well that's what he associated the noise with. Something horrible was coming this way. The cop was yelling into his phone out in the hall way.

Steven's handcuff was on his other wrist. The left wrist was wrapped in bandages. His fingers were still pruned, he could see blue under the skin of his hands.

"This is all your fucking fault!" the cop screamed from the door frame. "Mark's somewhere in the hospital. He left his room. Something happened to him." He pointed at Steven's hand, "Something like what's happenin' to you!"

He spun and ran down the hall as he cried "Nurse."

Steven looked down at his arm. He wasn't turning blue everywhere. It's not like a cold like a corpse. He only saw blue, very intense blue, especially where the thickest of his veins were. It was like the palm side of his wrist all over his arm.

He fell asleep. He dreamed. He dreamed that he found the cop next to the nurses station and ripped his head off. That he hit another guard with a part of his bed, it was some how attached to his wrist still.

He rushed outside. There was a mob there. Then the mob was running. He was eating something. It wasn't cooked and was a weird texture.

Mark, the Linebacker cop, was suddenly next to him. Mark

punched him.

Steven found himself covered in blood. In his right hand, was someone's arm. He was still dragging part of the bed on the handcuffs. Steven threw the arm and snapped off the handcuffs. He ran to the edge of the side walk and forced himself to throw up.

Mark was there. "Sorry about punching you. You needed to wake up. When we sleep, that happens." He pointed at the arm.

"What are we?" Steven asked, wiping blood from his mouth.

Mark shrugged, "I don't know. Right now, we're hunted. We can work together to survive though. I'm Mark."

Steven smile ruefully, "Nice to meet you, officially. I'm Steven."

Mark gave him a curt nod, "Right. I have a cabin up in the hills. Let's head there, get some supplies and then go somewhere deeper into the mountains."

"You though, you'll be sleeping on this leash. Others will find us, through you."

Steven dreamed in fits and starts of a mad dash into the mountains. When he woke next, he was surrounded by dozens of people just like him.

Mark glanced at him, "We've started something here. I'm glad you're awake to take part Steven. Something big is coming."

Steven didn't know if he should take comfort in that or be worried.

Arrogant Colonizers

Oh, i just must tell you, dear reader, about the latest discovery on
*****. You will simply delight about it. We've found intelligent life on
this horrendous planet, but like everything else, it's marvelously
confusing!

You know the pictures you've seen, of these adorable little things?
Well, reader, those are the "elders" as they care called. Which is
baffling to me, dear reader. They look childlike down right infantile!

However, according to the "productives" they are the repositories
of knowledge and wisdom. They are the, and get this reader, the past
and the future. Apparently, these childlike things, hold the collective
knowledge of generations, if you can believe that I have a bridge to sell
you.

I can tell you that giants did not, oh, no they did not, like when we
dissected one of those little things. Reader, I must confess, I truly did
fear for my life. If it wasn't for our noble Citizen Soldiers, why, I
probably wouldn't be here writing this to you my dear lovely,
brilliant reader.

I'm not even really sure why those giants got so upset about us
killing and cutting up one of these childlike things. I mean, it almost
immediately turned into a crystal. A crystal so hard that we couldn't
cut it with anything we had on hand. The Plasma torches just had all
their light and energy refracted or absorbed by the crystal.

Within a day or so the strangest thing happened, dear reader. The
crystal opened and a productive stepped out! They were one of the
largest and fully developed productive we have ever seen. It appears

that the natural radiation in the caves on ***** must provide the energy these strange beings need to mature and go through their life cycle.

Dear reader, I was lucky I wasn't present for the opening of that crystal. Everyone observing the crystal and making readings, in person, was immediately killed. I mourned for their loss dear reader. I mourned even more when that beautiful specimen had to be put down.

I know my dear reader, what you must be thinking. But fear not, the Productives are no more intelligent than the family dog. They only show glimmers of intelligence when there are a group of them. Then one becomes their leader. Otherwise, they are managed by one of those child like things.

So, like a vicious dog, we put that productive down. It was as beautiful and perfect as one of those things possibly could be. Unlikely the rabid beast that you can toss into a grave to rot and turn back into dust, these monsters aren't so gracious.

That productive turned into a crystal as well! We did everything we could to remove it from our campsite, dear reader. We discovered, to our horror, that the crystal developed a growth that broke through the camp's floor and found our power lines. We did our best to isolate the power from that room.

Dear reader, do you remember the comic books we read as a child? One that always brought me joy was the Hulk. I know, reader, that the Hulk is typically portrayed as a brutish stupid, simple monster. However, I enjoy it because of the complexity of the psychology of the character.

Well, reader, this giant, was very Hulk like. It was huge compared to the others we'd seen before. It was smarter than the other ones and it seemed to know how to get more power, which made it get larger.

Our camp was nearly destroyed, reader. I cannot believe such a being could possibly exist. It destroyed a number of tanks. Countless Citizen Soldiers. Fortunately, our Mech Suited Warriors managed to put the monstrosity down.

To our horror, the monstrosity spawned a dozen smaller crystals. We left before the monsters spawned again. Reader, I barely got off ***** alive. I think there can be only one solution to such a horrific place. We need to open a black hole at the center of the planet.

Dear reader, there can be NO mistaking it. Those monsters are a threat to our very survival. If they are able to create interstellar travel they will attack us. There will be no rational basis for their attack. They will seek to destroy us. They will simply drop a handful of productives and nuke them. leaving them to absorb the radiation and grow as large as they can.

Reader, our peaceful scientific exploration was met with unbridled fury. We were constantly attacked. We did nothing to them, yet we were always under guard.

I hope you take this warning to heart. Those monsters cannot be trusted.

– Transmission from Dr. Prof. John Smith, Lead Researcher on ***** specialist in Xenobiology

Emergency Landing

Everything is hopeless. Fuck it all.

Alarms blared. There's a hiss of air coming from somewhere in the cabin. Lights were flashing. The planet's surface was rapidly approaching. The baffling on the nose of the ship was on fire.

Sweat poured down her face. The other two were out cold. It's up to her. She doesn't know what to do. They're all going to die. There's nothing for it.

She looked at her hands. They were shaking. She closed her eyes and took a deep breath. The hissing didn't matter. That's a problem for after they land. The lights don't matter. She can see all the information she needed on the console.

The alarm. There are a lot of them. She pulled up the alarm console. Anything with leaks, she ignored. Then she moved on to the one that she could do something about. Speed.

The other two were out, because they were in a spin. Flatten out, then fix the spin. It wasn't just a spin, though. It was a tumble. Fix the spin then the yaw.

She grabbed the yoke and began to reduce that spin.

She fixed herself to a horizon and worked to force the ship to align to it. Minutes passed. The ship slowly lost its roll. The horizon stayed horizontal. Now it just rotated out the window.

Next, stop the rotation of the horizon. She pressed the pedals, slowing the rotation. This was harder, as one of the engines was blown. She idled the engine and used friction to slow the ship.

Her crew mates began to wake. They'd take over. She knew it.

They were still fucked, but at least they knew what they were doing.

"Wha? What's that noise?" Captain Magna asked.

She grunted in return. Straining to keep the ship under control.

"Holy shit, we're going to die!" Magna screamed. "What did you do? Carter answer me!"

Carter gritted her teeth, "I'm busy here you asshole. I know we're going to die. I'd rather do it after we land, though."

Lt. Soen groaned, "Stop the spinning, holy." He lurched to his feet, he tried staggering, somewhere. He was almost immediately thrown back into his seat. Which was for the best.

Carter finally stopped the rotation. The ship was slowing, which meant the air was hotter. The belly of the ship was blasting through the planet's atmosphere. It was a thick atmosphere. A lot more methane in the air than on Earth.

Magna regained his composure, "Let's get some more speed and get out of this heat. Ease the nose down."

Carter eased the nose down, struggling. The ship wanted to tumble. Sweat dripped onto her upper lip, she resisted the urge to blow it away.

"Soen, check the engine. Try to figure out what's going on with it." Magna ordered.

"That's her job though," Soen whined.

Magna fixed him a stern look, "Your job was to get us on the surface safely. She's doing your job, so do hers. If we land, we will discuss this behavior of yours. We're WASA, we do what we need to." Magna shook his head at Soen.

Carter felt the air thicken. Driving the heat back up. "Sir, we will have to deal with this heat at some point. We can't pick up much more speed. The farther down we go the thicker the air." She pulled the nose up, bleeding speed, but spiking the heat, immediately. "I'll bounce up and down, sir. Like a bird."

She took a breath and set herself to riding that line between heat and speed. She could see smoke trailing behind their ship.

"Sir," Soen interrupted her thoughts, "The engine isn't going to be useable. We'll have to do whatever we need to do with one engine."

A different pitched alarm spun up. Magna groaned, "Carter, find a place that looks like we might be able to crash our escape pod."

Carter laughed. There was a hysterical edge to it.

Soen cleared his throat. "Stop it." Carter continued to laugh. "STOP LAUGHING LIKE THAT!"

As they continue to bounce up and down, they flew over massive clouds of smoke. The clouds had drifted far from the source. There was a strong wind, certainly fueling the fire.

"My god, what is that?" Magna asked.

"Whatever hit us." Carter stated. She banked as gently as she could at those speeds.

There was a concentrated beam of energy blasting the surface of the planet. Smoke obscured sections of the beam and the surface.

Carter flew them past the beam and pointed the nose of the ship up the path of destruction.

"Only strip of land we might be able to survive impact. Everything else has trees or water." Carter said. Desperation plain on her face.

Magna nodded, "I don't like it. We don't have much choice though, do we?"

Soen was punching some commands on a keyboard. He looked at the other two and grimly nodded. "I've got a route entered into the escape pod. Hopefully we're low enough and slow enough to survive."

Carter punched some commands into the console while the other two prepped the escape pod.

"Come on Carter." Magna called over coms.

Carter hit enter on the keyboard, jumped up and sprinted to the pod. She could already feel the ship losing stability.

She dove into the pod. Magna slammed the door close button and the pod ejected from the ship. Carter felt weightless for a moment. She grabbed the seat harness and pulled herself in.

The view from the viewport was already tumbling. She was slammed into the seat as the stabilizing engines kicked on. The horizon settled.

She held on for dear life as the pod navigated the air currents. The smoke was incredibly hot, the pod was drifting on the temperature currents. Eventually it settled over the massive scar on the planet and found a place that was relatively safe to land.

The three crew members pulled themselves out of the ship. Carter collapsed onto the ground. She fell asleep immediately.

She felt a nudge on her side. She sat up. Her suit was covered in soot. The ground was an ashy burnt mess. She blinked and tried to focus on who had kicked her.

"Come on, get up. You've slept long enough." Magna grated. "Help us set up camp."

She dragged herself to her feet. A massive hab had already been set up. She went and pitched in.

"Near as we can tell," Soen began, "A solar eclipse caused the focused solar energy to tear grooves into the planet."

Carter looked at Soen, "What do you mean? Like the moon is a magnifying glass or something?"

Soen only shrugged in response.

Magna gave him a look, "Whatever it is, this isn't a safe long term location. If it is solar eclipses doing this, then this planet's ecology developed with that happening. For all we know, there's a continual solar eclipse moving across the planet. We're going to have to be careful. We'll be working in shifts. Carter, you already had your rest, so you'll be up for the next 16 hour. Soen, your turn to rest."

Soen grunted and went to his "room" in the hab. Chances were, they'd be hot bunking it. After he was gone, Magna patted Carter on the shoulder. "That was damn good work after we got hit. Soen and I were out for most of it, weren't we?"

Carter nodded. "Yea, we were all knocked out when we got hit by it." She blinked and rubbed her eyes. "Sir, I think we flew into the eclipse as it was just starting. I don't think Soen flew into a laser."

Magna chuckled, "I don't think he did either. The thing about eclipses though, they happen when the planet isn't behind the moon, too. We might not have been able to see it."

Magna leaned back, "Ultimately, it's my fault." He glanced about the hab. "I know you've been busy, but I'm sorry about Alex."

She sat backed stunned. She hadn't even thought about him, Gerald, or Christine. And those were just the other crew members. She looked up at him, "Shit."

She rushed out of the hab fell to her knees and cried. She cried so hard she threw up. She held her stomach as she bawled. She wiped her nose then wiped the snot onto her pants. She looked up at the sky.

It was dusk now. The stars were coming out.

Alex loved this time of night. Said it was the birth of something different, not the death of the day.

The sky glittered.

She felt a hand on her shoulder. She looked up at Magna. He spoke softly, "It's normal. Your reaction. Forgetting about everyone else. You're not a bad wife." He looked up at the sky forlornly. "It's overwhelming. I almost rather I died." Tears streaked down his face.

"Oh my god, your daughter was one of the passengers." Carter gasped, all she could smell or taste was ash.

Failed Prophesies

"Sir," Lt. Davey interrupted his thoughts, "We've captured the Golem. It had information we were seeking on it."

The Phoenix, he who was prophesized, rubbed his hands and stood. "Excellent!" He touched the Lieutenant , who managed to barely flinch as he stared at the wings tattooed on the back of those hands, "Let's go talk with The Golem!"

Lt. Davey lead the Phoenix down into the belly of the compound. It was an ancient fortress, one that had been used in days past to fight back the forces of the Dark One. It had taken the Phoenix a decade of fighting to reclaim it.

Lt. Davey unlocked the cell. It hummed with magical energy. The lock disengaged much of the shielding. Davey turned to The Phoenix, "Be on the ready, Sir. With the shield down, The Golem is a formidable foe. The cost was high. We lost a dozen Phoenix Guardians."

"A dozen?" The Phoenix replied softly. His voice choked with grief. "Give me the list immediately."

Davey provided The Phoenix the list. Davey studied the man. It was easy to forget how young this man was. The pressure of the prophesy had certainly aged the man, but he still looked no older than 30. While older than The Phoenix's actual age of 24, he was still a young man. The Phoenix mouthed each name as he read it. Setting it to his memory.

The Phoenix sighed, "That's well over a hundred this year, alone. We needed them. I'll sorely miss Guntel, he was a powerful mentor of mine."

The Phoenix wiped his eyes, "Let's go."

Lt. Davey lead the way into the cell. A giant hulk of a being fill most of the space. Massive chains pulled the limbs taut, leaving no room to flex. The Golem's head lulled. Purple fluid ran from its forehead. There were gashes across its abdomen.

"The Golem. I've been waiting to meet a general in the Dark One's army." The Phoenix said.

The Golem spat purple hued blood on the cell floor. Some stained the Phoenix's white robes. The being looked at them both. It's 3 sets of eyes allowing it to focus on both at once. "You simply had to look in your shaving mirror. Why involve me?" The Golem laughed.

Lt. Davey gestured towards one of the guards, who struck the Golem. The Golem's laugh sputtered into a hacking cough.

"I am destined to burn this world so it can live again. You understand that, right?" The Phoenix explained. The phoenix wings covering his hands shimmered with heat.

"The dark one is imprisoned there, you understand that, right?" The Golem spat back. "What world do you want reborn?!" The Golem cried.

"One without the Dark One." The Phoenix replied, his eyes glowing.

The Golem sighed. An exhausted look crossed his face. "Alvin, The Phoenix, do you know how many times this has played out before?"

"I am the fifth Phoenix." The Phoenix's eyes glowed.

The Golem gave a soft laugh, "I wish that were the case. You're the fifth of this age. The most successful of this age by a long shot. Each age is punctuated with a different attempt by the Dark One to escape. A new Prophecy to rekindle it. I have lived through 5 ages. You're the 60th Phoenix I've dealt with."

The Phoenix's wings sprouted from his back.

The Golem gave the Phoenix a rueful look, "Though, I expect you'll be my last." The Golem looked up, tears flowed down its face. "I did my best. It wasn't enough."

"You will tell me how to get through the gate. How to burn down the Dark One's prison, so I can destroy HIM."

The Golem looked at The Phoenix, "The gate?" It snorted. "I'm tired. So tired."

It's head dropped. Blood oozed out of its nose. A wracking cough contorted its body.

"Sir," A call came from the door. The Phoenix turned, it was Murray, his Prophet, "I've reread the Prophecy. It seems we could interpret it to say the Golem IS -"

The Golem screamed in pain. The being's body contorted and stretched. Lt. Davey could see a giant hand press against The Golem's ribs. Another pressed against its abdomen. The cut spread and peeled back.

The Golem shattered. The Dark One's prison was shattered. HE was free. The Phoenix launched into an attack. The Phoenix burned bright. He was brighter than he'd ever been before. Lt. Davey stepped back. Then ran from the cell. He cried for the Phoenix Guardians.

The Prophet grinned and called, "My Lord! You're free at last. I'm sorry it took so long."

The cell vibrated, "Time matters not. This world is mine now."

The Phoenix's flame suddenly snuffed out. He fell to the ground. Alvin slid into the inky blackness of the Dark One.

He screamed in pain. The darkness shrunk. Eventually all that remained was a dark cloudiness surrounding Alvin. He stood and shifted his shoulder. He turned to look at the Prophet. His eyes radiated a purplish black smoke. He opened his mouth, a void stared at anyone looking into the mouth, "Come, Alvin, let's rebuild this world."

Black flames licked the Phoenix tattoo as the Dark one burst through the fortress floor, out into his domain.

It had taken Audilum a year to set the world right. The world in his image. To fully replace the taint of the Creator. Everything was as Audilum dreamed. He had relished the total control. The domination. The ease at which he molded continents, seas, and peoples into which served him. Him and only him.

He, of course, did notice that a number of people, beings, and formations had suddenly disappeared. The Horn of Giants had just vanished. It had been the last strong hold against him. One day there was fierce resistance and then next, the gates were hanging open. Food still fresh on the tables. Fires still burning, but no one was there. No bodies, no mass suicide. The inhabitants were just gone.

Audilum knew the Creator had simply taken them. That Audilum had been powerless to stop the Creator. But the Creator had ceded this world to Audilum. That meant, there was another world for Audilum to conquer. There was still more.

There had to be more. More than this. Audilum looked down at his courts, for he many at once. In between sacrifices to his name, ritual orgies, and duels between great champions, there was arbitrating between farmers. He had originally willed food into being for his followers to eat, but he quickly grew bored of that. So he made a race of farmers. They were only able to farm. They ate what they farmed. They were easy to kill and plunder their crops. Which was fun for his generals to do. However, that meant they didn't fight and so they needed an arbiter over crop issues. It was exhausting, boring and did not fill Audilum with a sense of greatness.

"How is this world better than the world of old?" Alvin whispered.

"You're still back there?" mocked Audilum.

Audilum stood then. He was wreathed in a great bird of purple and black flames. "All farmer disputes will be settled with a game of Chem." He left his castles then. Reintegrating on the top of Mt. Audilum. The tallest mountain in the world.

He stood on top of the wind blown snow. The top of the mountain had never seen a blade of grass, even before, it had been a large mountain, before that a sea. Audilum looked up on his domain. He could feel the worship. He could see the prayers. He could read the scriptures and the temple sermons to be given. Everything was focused on him.

"Why is there so much suffering?" Alvin demanded.

"Because I will it."

"Even you grow bored with the tedium of banal suffering."

Audilum looked out into emptiness above his mountain. He searched, yet again, for where the creator had gone. Where his brothers and sisters had gone. Why didn't they fight to reclaim this world?

"I miss the stars." Alvin muttered sadly.

"The stars. They're gone." Audilum gasped.

Audilum launched himself into the void beyond the planet. He flew far into the nothingness. Beyond the moon, towards the sun.

He arrived at the sun. "Where did the other worlds go?"

"These stars are gone too." Alvin lamented.

Audilum stepped into the sun, he set himself ready. He wasn't really prepared to siege the sun, but he had no other choice. He sprinted forward. He found the gates of the golden city.

He manifested his power and blasted down the gates. They flew inward without resistance. Bouncing off their massive hinges useless on the great way beyond. The gates were unmanned. No one called out a challenge. No war horns sounded. Audilum walked through the city ready for something. his sense were stretched out, searching for anyone.

"They've all left you. You're all alone."

"I'm not alone. I have an entire world!" Audilum growled.

"An entire world and still alone." Alvin sighed.

Audilum screamed in rage. Then he felt it, a presence. He shot towards it. In the central castle, fortress, they flew. Straight through walls and buildings, with no regard for the destruction left in his wake. Audilum found himself in the throne room.

He had entered behind the throne. He could feel the warmth. The glow of the Creator.

He stalked around the chair. Fists held high, ready to strike or defend.

The being on the chair said "Welcome, my child. Though, you could have used the front door." There was a warm chuckle from the speaker.

"The Golem?!" Alvin gasped.

The figure resolved into the Golem, then transformed into something smaller, a fragile bent figure. He looked exhausted.

"Stoen," Audilum stated.

"Good to see both of you." Stoen smiled. "Though, let's set things right." he waved his hand and Audilum was pulled out of his body. Audilum looked down and saw his own body, not Alvin's. Alvin had fallen to his knees where Audilum had been standing.

"How DARE you-" Audilum screamed.

"Alvin is the only thing of mine left in this space. You made the earth, moon, and sun, do not forget." Stoen pointed a finger at

Audilum. He cut through the scream without raising his voice.

"I will take Alvin and you will have this world. This universe for your own. Grow it, expand it. Make new worlds." Stoen said, with a gentle smile.

"Why would you abandon this creation of yours?" Audilum asked plaintively.

Stoen shrugged, "I want you to be happy. If having this place as your dominion makes you happy. Then it's yours. I will leave it to you."

"How can you leave the suffering behind?" cried Alvin. "Those creatures suffer so much. You, you could do something about it. I thought I was serving you, I, I. What have I done?" Alvin sobbed.

"You've carried a heavy burden Alvin. You succeeded in created a reborn world. You thought you were doing the right thing. You were a good man with the wrong mission. You did it with honor and justice."

Audilum scoffed.

Stoen fixed him a hard look, "You scoff at him? He's the only being in eons that was able to break your bindings and you SCOFF!"

"Your Golem was tired." Audilum stated dismissively. "He even said so."

"He was tired because of Alvin. You owe him a debt. However, you never paid your debts. Just turned them into your advantage."

Stoen looked at Alvin, "You're right, was a lot of suffering in your world. Much of that is the fault of Audilum. His actions created the space for suffering. Ultimately, it's my fault. I couldn't create a perfect world. I tried. This was the best universe I could create. I created many worse. Even the world I moved your people to, has suffering. Without Audilum, the arc of justice is shortening and things are getting better."

"You, you blamed me all these years! You told me I RUINED IT! It was you!" Audilum said.

"Yes, I am flawed. If I was not, then I would never had said that. I'm sorry."

Alvin looked between the two great beings, "Huh, if Stoen leaves, the Creator leaves this place, doesn't that make you the Creator, Audilum. Can't you make a better creation than your father? Couldn't you make your own children to share the work?"

Stoen coughed, "That's pretty much what I did with my father."

"Your father?" Audilum and Alvin asked in unison.

Stoen laughed.

Audilum groaned in exasperation.

"Maybe things would have gone differently if you hadn't been alone, Stoen. Audilum," Alvin stood tall, "I want to help you rebuild this world. I want to balance your..." he hesitated and glanced at the purple and black flames wreathing Audilum, "your darker and dramatic tendencies."

"I was the source of all your power before. You can't do anything without me."

Alvin wreathed himself in bright blue tinged in red flames. A filtered mirror to Audilum. Light to his dark. "You've left something of yourself in me."

Stoen raised his hand, "No, this wasn't something I did. I didn't pull you out of yourself. I couldn't. I haven't had that power over you in a very long time."

Audilum took a deep breath and reached out. He found no difference himself. He reached out to Alvin, there was a different type of power there. A partnered power.

Audilum touched Stoen. Found a blend of the two powers in him. Audilum opened his eyes. He nodded, "Fine. Let the two of us rebuild this world. One with less suffering. One where there's no dark one trapped and locked away. One where Justice and Vengeance work hand in hand."

Alvin turned to Stoen, "I may have been yours, but I am no more. You have no attachment to this world any longer. You are free to leave."

Stoen smiled. Age seemed to melt from him, "Oh thank you for taking this burden. I wish you both the best of luck." He winked and vanished.

Alvin and Audilum looked at each other, then back at the throne.

"I'll make another one," Alvin said.

Fell Jack and the Fallen Empire

Fell Jack wiped blood from his chin. He rose to unsteady knees. He spat blood at Too Tall Trall.

Trall laughed, "Did you think I'd just, give it to you?" He rushed back towards Fell Jack axes high.

Fell Jack glanced to his left, it was clear enough for him to roll. He readied his dagger. Too Tall Trall bore down on Fell Jack. He threw an axe just before he arrived.

Jack smiled as he rolled out of the axe's way and threw his dagger back at Trall. It wasn't his strongest throw, it glanced off leather and rib. It wouldn't slow down Trall much.

As soon as Fell Jack caught his footing, he lunged back towards Too Tall Trall, pulling a knife from his boot. Trall turned towards Jack only to get tackled by Jack. Jack heard the whoosh of Trall's breath. Jack took advantage of his brief advantage to stab Trall in the chest rapidly in a few quick movements.

Fell Jack picked up Trall's thrown axe, while keeping an eye on the man. Trall was gasping for breath. Blood seeped through fingers pressing against his wound. Jack feinted, Trall jerked his axe into a groin level swing. Jack quickly stepped around and severed Too Tall Trall's head.

With jagged breath Fell Jack grabbed Trall's other axe. He set himself, waiting. A rough semicircle had formed around the two men. The rest of his men, bastards one and all, wanted his payment too.

There was a sudden roar of approval behind Fell Jack. He stood between their patron, Tyrant Black Fang, and the rest of his men.

"Great sport, Fell Jack! You always knew how to make an entrance. It's a shame about your man, though. He would have made a great showing at the tournament today."

Fell Jack turned and bowed. "Thank you my lord. I'm sure you understand, rule through strength and prowess."

"Certainly, young man. With an iron fist. Come now. Your payment. The sword for you and GOLD, more GOLD than your men could drink in a lifetime."

"My men are quite thirsty, my lord."

"Killing is thirsty work. There's more to be done, if you're interested."

Fell Jack turned to his men, "Do you want to paid in gold and blood, men?"

His men roared.

Fell Jack slammed the axe in the corpse of Too Tall Trall and walked to Tyrant Black Fang. He could hear the men spitting on Trall's corpse behind him.

Fell Jack was roughly searched by a member of White Paw, the Tyrant's personal guard. He was relieved of a number of daggers and his favorite eating knife. He was pushed forward, towards the Tyrant.

Tyrant Black Fang drew Ulilin. It shimmered as the fire light danced across it's oily surface. "They say, the true wielder of this sword cannot be killed by it. That's a misunderstanding of the prophecy, though. I believe a more correct reading of the prophecy is that the true wielder will not stay dead."

He turned his golden eyes towards Fell Jack. He had a wolfen face, like all of his people. He had a glistening white fang and a matte black fang that seemed to exude blackness. Jack had the misfortune of seeing these fangs, because Tyrant Black Fang was smiling and to see one of the True People smiling, was death.

"Do you, Fell Jack, believe you are the TRUE Wielder of Ulilin?"

Arms roughly grabbed Jack from behind.

"FUCK YOU!"

He felt the fabled fire of the meteor in the sword burn his life away. He fell away. The world grew small, as the meteor took him for a ride.

He felt the sword drink life from thousands of men, women, and children. Each time, the sword cried out for a hand worthy of wielding it. Eventually, the sword turned on all who used it. A slip here landing on the sword. A sudden shift in weight there just missing a parry.

Fell Jack saw the destruction the meteor wrought when it cashed to earth. An ancient city, devastated. It's whole history was one of calamity and betrayal.

Then he saw worlds and stars he could never imagine. He felt a yearning; a need to return to the great emptiness above. Into the great beyond.

Every time it tasted a death on its edge, Ulilin returned to that emptiness for a moment.

The sword pulled out of Fell Jack. He fell to his knees, following his heart's blood. He retched then fell face down.

He was in the tent and riding in the meteor's wake. He flew past giant planets, made of gas. Passed through the birth place of stars, he stirred up the gas, triggering the formation of what could be a planet or star in a million years.

He didn't need breath in the void. He didn't need blood or a beating heart in the great emptiness. Why did he in the tent? He only need to be with Ulilin.

Fell Jack crawled back to his knees. He looked at the Tyrant, "You have my sword."

Tryant Black Fang took a step back. His hackles rose. He growled.

Fell Jack opened his hand and Ulilin was there. He felt vigor return to his body. Blood pounded in his heart. His wound was gone.

Ulilin was moving in his hand of its own accord. He found himself spinning, disemboweling the two White Paws that had held him and let Black Fang kill him. They dropped their swords as they clutched their stomachs. They died noisily.

"Stop. I Command you." Tyrant Black Fang said.

Fell Jack moved to clean Ulilin, only to notice, the sword had drank the blood. Something hit his foot, he glanced down to see the sword's sheath.

"Sheath Ulilin. Now!" Tyrant whined.

Fell Jack could feel Tyrant collecting his power. The sword told Jack that now wasn't the time. Jack wasn't ready for this fight yet. The time will come. Jack will claim this world. Would set Ulilin back out into the void.

Fell Jack sheathed the sword and added the weapon to his belt.

He took back his other daggers and his favorite eating knife back from the corpse at his feet. After putting everything in order he finally turned to Tyrant Black Fang.

"You betrayed me. I will remember that. Have your White Paw deliver gold to my men. Double what you promised me."

Tyrant Black Fang snarled. "No. I'll give you what I promised. You and your men will be paid in advance, the same amount, to go conquer Antina."

Fell Jack smiled, "Antina, huh? Spoils will be ours. I will be Governor of Antina. For you, my Lord."

"Fine. I'll be sending a White Paw with you. She will be my voice in all things. Especially, where you go after Antina."

Jack snorted.

"I know you plan to follow the prophesy, because you will be compelled. I want to make sure you do it with my interpretation of it. She has a deep knowledge of these things."

"So be it." Fell Jack spat on his hand and held it out.

Tyrant Black Fang sighed in disgust, he licked his paw and shook.

"Bring Short Snout to Fell Jack." Black Fang called to his guards. "Councilor Leona, pay him."

Fell Jack left the command tent. His men were anxiously waiting outside. He raised the sword and cried, "I am the TRUE WIELDER! We march to Atina!"

His men roared.

Fell Jack could hear Ulilin singing.

An Unlived Life

The man blinked. He glanced around his living room. It was a snug space. Gas fire in the fire place, his easy chair pointed towards its it. The ice in his whiskey clinked as he glanced about. Something was off.

He heard it, a slight pop and click. He glanced at the record player on the table next to the mantle. The record was finished. He grunted as he stood. His knee popped. He pulled the needle from the record and pressed the stop button. He double checked, he was on side D.

He grunted to himself. He shook his head as he picked up the record sleeve and quickly put the record into the sleeve. He slid that into the record cover and shuffled to his collection of vinyls. He slid this one back into place and looked across the genres in his collection. He picked one from the classic rock section. When he'd bought the records they had already been tattered and beaten. That was 50 years ago. The band he picked, Steely Dan, wasn't one most people remembered today.

He put it on. It fit his mood.

He shuffled across the room as the music played. This album had significantly more hissing and popping than the last one. Of course that album had been bought new 40 years ago.

He stepped into his kitchen. He sighed as he settled into the ritual of making coffee.

As Reelin' in the Years continued to play, he'd inadvertently started on the B side. He looked at his coffee set up. It was nearly 30 years old. He'd refreshed pieces as he needed, but it'd keep going.

These rituals were all that kept him together. The rituals were the only control he had in his life. Picking the record, loading it, starting it up. Weighing the beans, boiling water, grinding beans, making coffee to a recipe. Noting the process and result. He had dozens of books devoted to recipes.

It wasn't much of a life wasn't it? Alone in this basement. He could control this world. Everything outside was chaos and dangerous. He directly poured the coffee into a thermos, not his favorite way of drinking, but he'd have to venture outside, so a thermos was a must.

He finished his coffee and shuffled to the record player. He popped the needle up. Then grabbed his "oh shit bag" and went outside coffee in hand.

He was masked. Which got looks. The world was in a pandemic lull and some of the kids were lucky enough to have never lived in a pandemic. It wasn't for the pandemic. The mask was a necessity to go outside.

It was a beautiful day. The sun was shining. Not a cloud in the sky. He popped on his eBike. He could have taken a cab or something else, but the bike was one of his few exercise sources.

He pedaled slowly, but moved quickly. The bike was great that way. He smiled, just enjoying the ride. The city had changed a lot over the years. After the big one hit, the city reshaped itself, ensuring resiliency to the next big one or a volcano erupt or rising sea levels.

He pedaled along. The road was busy, but without the cars of the early 21st century, it was quiet and relaxing to be on the road. Eventually his ride ended. He locked up the bike and shuffled into his allergists office. He went through the routine of checking in. Though, they knew who he was. They tolerated his mask much more than the outside world.

He was called back to meet with his doctor. He blinked when she walked in the room.

She laughed, "Yep! I got it. A full body replacement."

He grunted.

"You know you're eligible. We've gotten approval for you." She said.

He squirmed, "Did the other you die? How did that work?"

"They did a full transfer. We've been over this. The other body doesn't survive the transition. Look, you need to do this. You're top on the list. You've lost decades of your life. You need to do this. None of our treatments have helped you. This is the cure."

"Fine." He said heavily. "Give me the number and I'll call them."

She sadly shook her head, "No, I've already made an appointment for you. It's later today."

"What? No! I have things I need to do this afternoon!"

She gave him a sad smile, one he'd seen for decades. "This is what's best for you."

He sat in angry silence for the rest of the appointment. He got his shots and then rode home.

He could feel his throat tighten as he got closer to his home. Next he smelled the smoke. He pulled up to his house. It was in flames. The fire department was already there, working to put it out.

He'd have to move, even if they saved it.

His vision narrowed. His eyes widened. He grabbed some pills from his bag. He took one and turned his bike to ride away. He started to sway. His heart raced. His mind slowed as he struggled to keep the bike moving.

He swerved onto the main road.

He woke up in pain. His body hurt everywhere. His head was immobilized. He couldn't feel his left leg. His right left was a line of fire below the knee.

He coughed.

"Oh, good you're awake." An unfamiliar voice said. "This isn't normally how we like to do these transfers. The fire alone, after your allergy shots, was almost enough to kill you. The driver of the car that hit you, thought for sure you were dead. You are a tough old man."

He grunted. He wasn't sure if it was agreement, pain, or annoyance. He found it was difficult to speak.

"Yea, you've got a broken jaw, skull, fibula and tibia, both arms, and your hip. We also had to amputate your left leg." The man sighed.

"Sorry, I forgot to introduce myself. I'm Dr. Alvarez." Dr. Alvarez stood and loomed into his line of sight. "Look, sir, Medicare has done the calculations and you have two options. Take the Younger You treatment or pay for your care on your own. I recommend taking the treatment."

Dr. Alvarez left him to his thoughts. He thought about everything he'd lost. How his world continued to shrink. His rituals where all he'd had left and now those were gone, tainted or poisoned. His mind in this prison were literally all he had left. Still, he didn't want to die, even if a version would wake up immediately. It meant a version didn't wake up. That was terrifying.

He glanced up. There was a TV placed up there for him. It was semitransparent, but still he could see himself. He was a mess. A disaster. His body a broken jumble of its past self. What would life even be in a shattered AND broken body. The prison walls had tightened farther.

He felt tears roll down his cheeks. Consent had been stripped from him. It was basically die from loss of home and injuries or do this transfer. It's not a choice. Consent can't be given. Only coercion. Only force.

He drifted in and out of consciousness. Eventually, he felt a presence. Dr. Alvarez was there, checking his vitals.

"Are you going to take the Treatment then?"

The TV above flashed to life with a "consent" form. It'd already been signed. His estranged wife had signed. She still had power of attorney. He groaned glaring at it. The TV registered that as a set of initials.

She'd already used the process. He sighed then. Resigned to his fate, he collapsed in on himself. He tried to force himself to sleep.

The next day Dr. Alvarez and some support staff wheeled him into a room. There was some equipment. Something that looked to go over his head. That was what did it.

He grunted. The nurse stopped to check if he was alright. He just glared at her. She sighed as she continued to fit him with the fixture.

"He's a grumpy man isn't he," She muttered to Dr. Alvarez.

"He's been through a lot. Plus, he's thought too much about this. His allergist gave me a run down of his thoughts on this. In a way, this," Dr. Alvarez gestured towards the old man's current condition, "is a blessing. He really had no choice."

He made a straining sound. Then started to laugh. It was a tortured sound.

Dr. Alvarez patted the old man's chest. It hurt like hell. The old man whimpered. "Your suffering will be over soon."

He found himself in a darkroom. His neck was hurt. He was a child, crying. He vaguely remember his brother pushing him out of bed. Suddenly, he was lost in a swamp. Then he was playing soccer. he was at a school dance. The memories came faster and faster. Stories he'd read. Stories, he'd watched. Things he learned. Stories he'd written. He saw them all.

It was so fast. Too much. He'd had so much life for so long. He just didn't realize it. Was too depressed and too reactive to truly enjoy it. Then his life became a series of continual loss and rituals. A life of grieving and terror.

He woke up in terrible pain. He body was destroyed still.

The nurse pointed at him, she screamed, "The body, its eyes are moving! ohmygod, ohmygod, ohmygod. What's happening?"

Dr. Alvarez looked grim. "Old man, You're too durable for your own good. Your younger self is meeting your estranged wife. He's meeting your allergist, who's going to verify your allergies are gone."

A nurse ran into the room. She was sheet white. Dr. Alvarez ran out of the room. There was sobbing and crying in the other room.

His estranged wife was there, "Did you stop this? You stubborn fool!"

All he could do is grunt. He fell asleep. He couldn't help it.

He suddenly found himself in that dark room again. Alone and frightened. There were two of him though. The other looked younger, thinner, somehow.

He reached out to the younger him, "It's ok. You're going to be OK."

"Are you sure? I don't want to be alone any longer."

"No, I don't know it's going to be OK. You won't be alone though. You can go out and be a whole person again. You can leave this dark painful prison behind." The old man said.

The young man wiped a tear, "But, you'll be gone?"

"Maybe that's for the best. Maybe this world doesn't need a broken bitter old man. A man so wrapped up in his rituals that he lost the only thing important to him."

The young man reached out and pulled the old man into a hug. "You've changed before. You can do it again. You spent years healing.

You gave up. You can keep going. Look around you, everyone is amazed that you keep going. You can change. You can grow."

The old man looked at the younger version of himself. "We can change, we can grow." His mind's eye blurred, shifted, and brightened.

He opened his eyes. There was no pain. He was laying in an empty room, well, there was one other person in it. His allergist. He coughed.

"Dr. Alvarez," She called, "come here!"

Alvarez, the nurse and other support staff rushed in. "We're trying to resuscitate him over there. He just –" He looked at the young man on the table in surprise.

"How, what," Alvarez sputtered.

The young man gave a rueful laugh, "I had some things I needed to sort out, I guess."

"How do you feel?" his allergist asked.

He looked at her, "Did you ever do Psilocybin? I feel like I just did an intense therapy session with that."

His estranged wife rushed up and hugged him. She gave him a kiss. "I've missed this. I've missed you."

"Our house is gone." He said.

She nodded, tears in her eyes, "Don't worry about it, Tim. I've already got everything sorted out."

He nodded. He's body felt loose relaxed. Most importantly, he didn't feel any anaphylaxis.